FRIENDS WITH BENEFITS

A DIFFERENT KIND OF LOVE NOVEL

LIZ DURANO

Friends with Benefits Copyright © 2018 by Liz Durano

Cover Design by James at GoOnWrite.com

Published by Velvet Madrid

All rights reserved. No part of this publication may be reproduced, distributed, or scanned in any printed or electronic form without permission. Please do not participate in or encourage piracy of copyrighted materials in violation of the author's rights. This is a work of fiction. Names, characters, businesses, places, events, and incidents are either the products of the author's imagination or used in a fictitious manner. Any resemblance to actual persons, living or dead, events or establishments is purely coincidental.

v. 2019_09_12

FRIENDS WITH BENEFITS

I've known Campbell Murphy all my life. He's the boy next door and my brother's best friend... the one man outside of family whom I can be completely myself with.

But when I wake up in his bed the morning after his company holiday party, there are two things I suddenly can't ignore:

One, Campbell Murphy is all grown up in more ways than one, and two, I no longer want to be *just* his best friend's sister.

What's even better is that we're on the same page...

But even if we end up not working out, is a fling worth sacrificing a lifetime of trust between families? Or is it worth a shot at something that had always been there all along?

Each book in *A Different Kind of Love* series is a STANDALONE story with NO cliffhanger and a guaranteed HEA. Some are angsty and emotional while some are fun and lighthearted... like this one!

A DIFFERENT KIND OF LOVE SERIES
FREE IN KINDLE UNLIMITED

Everything She Ever Wanted: Dax and Harlow (Book 1)

Falling for Jordan: Addison and Jordan (Book 2)

Breaking the Rules: Sawyer and Alma (Book 3)

Every Breath: Sarah and Benny (Book 3.5)

Friends with Benefits: Caitlin and Campbell (Book 4)

Every Good Thing: Roxy and Kodi (Book 4.5)

"Love isn't always pretty and rich, sometimes it earthy and hard-won." - Carly Quinn, author of *Solitude* and *Kawaipuna Cottage*

to my Lucas.

ONE

Caitlin

I see him in the crowd, a head taller than everyone else around him, his familiar grin reminding me that he's not just my older brother, he's my best friend, too. And boy, have I missed him.

"Jory!"

I leap into his arms like I used to when we were kids. Only this time, I'm all grown up and from the way Jordan takes a step back to regain his footing the moment I land in his arms, I'm probably also too big to pull the same stunt year after year. But it's not like he's ever minded before.

"Whoa, sis!"

Until now.

Jordan sets me down on the ground and steps back, surveying my outfit. Five hours on the plane meant I had to be comfortable so a long-sleeve shirt and yoga pants were in order.

"Mom was right. She said you wouldn't bring a coat... or a scarf, for that matter," he says, laughing. "Come on, Cait, what is this flimsy little thing?"

The 'flimsy little thing' is a thin faux leather jacket I picked up a discount store in LA. "It was seventy degrees when I left."

"Well, you're home now and it won't hit seventy for another four months." Jordan lifts the wool coat he'd slung over his arm. "It's projected to be in the 30's here. Hopefully it will snow."

"Oh, good! Then I can beat you in the snowball fight we're gonna have like I always do," I say, laughing as he helps me into my coat and then wraps a scarf around my neck for good measure.

"Ha ha, Cait. Dream on," he says. "Did you check in any luggage?"

I shake my head. "Nope, just my carry-on and that's it."

As I follow my older brother through the crowd, I can't believe I'm finally home, even if it's only for three weeks. I've had a tough semester so far and I've been looking forward to this moment for months. There's no other place I'd rather be for Christmas—with family— and it's always been the same all my twenty-five years.

The only exception would be last year when Jordan

spent the holidays in the Philippines building schools and clinics for a nonprofit. All we got was a phone call wishing us a Merry Christmas and I was gutted. I hated seeing everyone at the dinner table except him but he was doing what he'd always wanted to do, travel the world while doing some good... although technically, he was also getting away from ex-girlfriend Rachel who refused to accept they were over.

The moment he got back nine months ago, I took three days off to fly back home just to see him and make him promise me never to miss Christmas again. After all, family is family.

Now he's got a family of his own and they're all spending Christmas Eve at the house. Who knew that just before he flew to Southeast Asia two years ago, he'd end up meeting his soulmate? Addison Rowe is a nephrology specialist with a private practice in Manhattan, and together they're parents to my most adorable niece and my parents' first grandchild, Piper. Long story short, basically Jordan had a one-night stand, but if ever there was a love story that was meant to be, it's theirs. And I love Addison to bits. She's funny and her mother makes the meanest fried egg rolls and pancit this side of the Mississippi.

As we make our way out of the terminal, I take in the sights and sounds of New York that I've missed so much. It doesn't matter that it includes honking cars, the smell of exhaust, and irate drivers. I'm just glad to be home again.

"Where are Addison and Piper?" I ask as I follow Jordan through the crowd. At six-feet-four-inches of solid muscle, he manages to clear the path just by being there.

"They're waiting at the house. You should see Piper, Cait. She's a little tornado, walking already and keeping Addy busy. Heck, she's keeping all of us on our toes. Who knew a baby could cause so much havoc?"

"The good kind of havoc, I hope?"

Jordan shoots me a look. "Of course."

I laugh. At twenty-nine, Jordan is the perfect father and it's no surprise. He was always protective of me when we were kids to the point that no one could ask me out without going through him first. And no one messed with the high school quarterback or his best friend, Campbell Murphy who took over whenever Jordan wasn't around.

We get to Jordan's truck ten minutes later. As he loads my luggage in the rear cab, I get in the passenger seat and set the heater to maximum. He was right. It's cold.

"So how's Campbell?" I ask as he gets behind the wheel and starts the engine.

"I think he's in Seattle, something about a due diligence meeting with potential clients, that kind of thing," he replies. "But he should be back by tomorrow, I think."

"I sure hope he got Christmas off."

"Of course, he did," Jordan says, grinning. "He may work a lot but the guy knows when to chill. You should see him play golf every chance he gets."

"I'm sure his bosses play it."

Jordan laughs. "You know they do. But Campbell actually enjoys it. He keeps threatening to introduce me to it as soon as the weather allows."

"I can't wait to see him again."

"I'm sure he'd be happy to see you, too, Cait."

While both guys are tight like guy friends go, Campbell is my friend, too, although these days, our phone calls have been replaced by text messages. But with him working as a hedge fund analyst and me completing my Masters in Molecular Biology in California, we do the best we can. Jordan and I have known him ever since he and his family moved in next door to us when I was four and Mom and Dad even consider him the unofficial third O'Halloran sibling. He has a seat at the table every holiday and any time he wants to stop by. Mom even knit him his own stocking which she hangs from the mantelpiece next to Jordan's and my own.

"I missed hanging out with him the last time I came home a few months ago," I say. "I think he was in the Bahamas or something."

"Saint Lucia."

"Lucky him."

"For work," Jordan adds.

"Still lucky him." I sigh. "Can you imagine being in Saint Lucia for work?"

"Yeah, I can imagine it, but don't forget, Cait. Campbell works twelve-hour days most times," Jordan says. "But when he parties, he parties."

"That's right. He does, doesn't he?" I laugh, remembering how he ended up having his pictures posted on Instagram after he ended up dating some social media celebrity. "I really hope I get to hang out with him this time. I need to do some serious partying to balance out all the research I've been doing for my dissertation."

As if in response, my phone vibrates and I see my best friend's name on the display. "Shit, I forgot to text Roxy that I've landed."

"Wish her Merry Christmas for me, will you?" Jordan says as I click answer. "I've been pretty out of the loop lately to know what she's been up to."

I laugh. "Ya think? You've got a wedding to plan, Jory. Your bar-hopping days are over."

"So when did you get in?" A high-pitched voice asks when I slip my earbuds on. I've known Roxy Porter since high school and whenever I come home, she and I usually hang out.

"We got in twenty minutes ago. Right now we're stuck in traffic. What's up?"

"Remember that party we went to the last time you were here? Well, one guy asked me about you and wanted to know if you're available to hang out."

"What did you tell him?" Roxy introduces me to a lot of people whenever I return home for a few weeks. After a while, the guys' faces and personalities blend together. She also knows I don't have time to date but she still fixes me up on dates anyway.

"Nothing. Anyway, his name's Malcolm. He's an investment banker and he drives a Porsche. You met him at Lindsay's party," she replies, unfazed. "He's this uber hot, blond god who happens to remember you and wants to take you with him to his company holiday party. I'll be there, too, which is good because if things turn south, I'll have your back."

"Who are you going with?"

"Jace. He's working the bar that night so I get to hang out as his assistant. Who knows? Maybe I'll even get tips. Bankers tip good, right?"

I laugh. "I have no idea, but maybe they will. It's the holidays, after all."

"Drunk people usually are more generous," she says. "So is it a yes?"

I don't want to commit just yet, not when Jordan is

eavesdropping. "Can I let you know tomorrow? I have to check my schedule. My family could have plans."

"There are still five days before Christmas, Cait, which means that's five days of partying."

I chuckle. "I'll let you know tomorrow."

"Alright. Anyway, I can't wait to let you try my latest accomplishment. Sex with the Bartender."

"You're already having sex with the bartender, Roxy. What's new?"

She laughs. "No! I mean the drink. It's one of the best things out there and so I've been practicing. Let's see... Malibu Coconut Rum, Bailey's Irish cream, Triple sec, 7-up, Grenadine, and Roses Lime Juice. See? I even know the ingredients. You should try it, Cait. I'll make you one at the party if you come."

Roxy has been dying to learn how to mix drinks for years. For a registered nurse, it's the last thing I would have thought about her but it's her way of relaxing after twelve-hour shifts in the ICU. While other people love to cook, she likes to mix drinks.

"We'll talk more about it tomorrow, Rox."

"So you going to the party?" Jordan asks after I say goodbye to Roxy and hang up.

"I don't know if I am or not yet. I promised one of my accountability partners at school that I'd–"

"Scaredy cat," Jordan coughs out the word and I whack his bicep playfully, although there's nothing playful about my glare. "Alright, alright. I was just kidding," he protests. "What happened with that Kieran guy you were seeing a few months ago?"

"We only dated for two months," I reply. "All he wanted to do was hang out at the cool spots so he could possibly run into some producer to pitch his next screenplay. It got old."

"I bet," Jordan says. "So how's school?"

I lean back against the seat, grateful for the topic change. My dating life is abysmal, not when I'm on a scholarship for my Masters and I don't want to blow it. "One more semester and I'll be done."

"What are your plans after that? Any plans for a vacation? You've always wanted to go to Italy."

"With what, Jory? My good looks? I need to work and start paying my way for a change. I'm twenty-five, for crying out loud. Even Roxy's working as a nurse now and she makes good money."

"And? It's not like you were slacking the entire time. You're in school... earning a Master's degree at that," he says. "Just remember to take a break, alright? Life isn't all about school and work, sis."

"I know, Mr. I-Spent-A-Whole-Year-Abroad-Building-Schools-While-Exploring-The World," I say as Jordan responds by rolling his eyes. "Anyway, I do have a few job prospects after graduation."

"East Coast, I hope?"

"No, most of them are West Coast, unfortunately. One is in Portland and the other is in Texas. With the job market being so tough these days, you can't really be too picky although I do hope I find something closer to home. I miss the four seasons. The fall colors, especially... and a white Christmas. I miss you guys most of all. It sure can get lonely out there in LA."

Jordan squeezes my hand. "We miss you, too, Cait."

Twenty minutes later, we make it to the O'Halloran family home in Forest Hills Gardens. It's a borough in Queens and about nine miles to Manhattan. The best word I could probably describe it is quaint although Roxy likes to call the neighborhood posh. And she might just be right. It's certainly different from the rest of the boroughs.

Thanks to Grosvenor Attenbury, the architect behind the Tudor-style homes that boast towers, Norman-style turrets, red-tiled clay and gabled roofs, Forest Hills Gardens often looks like an English village when people first stumble upon it. Some streets even have wrought iron streetlights on top of "Harwich Port blue" lampposts. Campbell used to live next door but it's changed hands since then. Right now, it's dark, the family living there choosing to spend their holidays in Florida year after year. They could, at least, hire someone to decorate it so it matches the neighborhood.

My excitement builds the moment Jordan parks the

truck in the driveway and I get out. The house exterior is bedecked with lights and I can only imagine the electricity bill. But it doesn't matter. It's gorgeous, as if celebrating my official return home for the holidays.

Mom and Dad are standing on the other side of the door and the moment I walk inside, it's utter mayhem. The smells of freshly baked chocolate chip cookies and hot chocolate make my mouth water as I lose myself in hugs and kisses from Mom, Dad, Addison and Piper. There's nothing like being home for Christmas and as I walk into the living room with Piper in my arms, I sigh at the sight of the Christmas tree.

The Fraser Fir is set up in the far corner of the living room and partially decorated only because that's what we're doing tonight. It's why everyone is here, to put up their respective ornaments that mark every year we've lived in this house.

The ornaments range from cheesy to classy to handmade projects from Jordan and my preschool years. I used to be embarrassed about them but now that I'm older, I'm grateful that Mom saved them all. Even Campbell has his commemorative ornaments, too, tucked in the storage box next to Jordan's and mine. Too bad he's not here to join us.

I hand Piper back to Addison as Mom reappears from the kitchen with a mug of steaming hot chocolate. Dad follows right behind her with a tray of cookies.

From the corner of my eye, I see Jordan standing next to Addison. They're both beaming like the proud parents that they are, and I feel a pang of jealousy hit me right in the chest, a yearning to find the same thing they've found in each other, true love. And to think they found it when they weren't exactly looking.

Sometimes I wonder if I'll ever allow myself to fall in love, but that thought only lasts for a few seconds, before the thought of my next dissertation hits me like a ton of bricks and I return back to earth. After everything Mom and Dad have sacrificed to get me all the way to grad school, I owe it to them to be successful. So, no, I don't have any time for love, not until after I graduate and then get a job and pay them back. Love can come later.

TWO

Campbell

I shouldn't be tired but I am. I've been up since four in the morning testing quantitative models for the team and wrapping everything up before I take the rest of the week off. It doesn't mean I'm going to be completely on vacation, though. I'm sure I'll still be working. I just won't be showing my face at the office.

Right now, the holiday party is rocking with free drinks flowing from the bar and everyone I know taking their selfies in front of the window that features a view of the Empire State Building lit up in holiday colors. Too bad everyone's still discussing business, especially with the boss having just left for the rest of the year. Who got a bonus? How much? As if someone would disclose their bonuses unless they're assholes wanting everyone to know just how important they are.

I glance at my watch. Only nine o'clock, still too

early to leave. But even if I went straight home, I'd probably still be working on statistical analysis and risk modeling or playing one of my roleplaying games with online friends based around the world. I do have to text Caitlin back. Maybe she and I could hang out since she's home for the holidays.

I finish my drink, something Roxy made for me that's actually pretty good. Apparently, she's dating some bartender and is now tagging along with him and learning how to mix drinks herself. She's one of Caitlin's friends but we're not close. She did try to hook me up with two of her friends but I just couldn't find a free slot in my busy schedule. Besides, I had no need for blind dates then or now. I find my dates fine on my own. Still, Roxy's pretty cool for an ICU nurse and wanna-be bartender.

"I hear you're off the rest of the year. You flying off somewhere warm? Saint Lucia maybe with one of your side chicks?"

I turn to see Marissa from Legal standing next to me, a tall glass of what looks like her third Long Island Iced Tea in her hand. I've no doubt she's already drunk. A lot of the employees are.

"Nah, I'm staying in town."

She looks at me in surprise. "I would have thought you'd be in the Caribbean by now, enjoying a Mai Tai or something, usually with some gorgeous model."

"Where'd you get such an idea?"

"I saw it on Instagram," she says as I scoff. "You get around for a shy boy, you know, so we at Legal made a bet that you'd probably show up on Insta again."

"Hope you didn't bet too much." I peer at her. She's definitely drunk, although she's right. I ended up seeing someone who turned out to be some social media celebrity but that was about it. I didn't even know anyone could do such a thing for living. At first, being around them was exciting, but the novelty wore off as soon as I realized that she and her friends turned everything into a social media opportunity.

"By the way, congratulations on being named one of the top twenty best analysts in the country. That's a huge accomplishment!" She grips my arm as she totters on her high heels. "I can't believe you and Carter made the list. As if we haven't gotten tired hearing about it from him every day. He framed the page and it's right there on his desk. What did you do with your copy?"

"It's in my desk drawer somewhere." I cross my arms in front of me and lean against the wall. I don't really want to talk about business. "What about you, Marissa? Going away?"

"Yup, a few days with family in Delaware for Christmas," she replies. "Got any family out here?"

"Extended," I reply, realizing it's probably the first time Marissa and I have ever talked about family. It's simply something we never discuss at work, too busy with deadlines. She'd just get bored if I told her the truth, that for the last three years, my mother spends the holidays with my stepdad in Florida where it's warmer and better for her arthritis. The rest of the year, she and Warren live in a renovated flat in Brooklyn. As for my father, who the hell knows where he is. I haven't heard from him ever since he left us when I was sixteen. I feel my jaw clench, my anger building. *Whatever, Dad.*

My thoughts are suddenly interrupted when I see Malcolm Carter walk in and my heart skips a beat the moment I see who he's with. Flaming red hair - check. Wide, perfect smile - check. Holy hell, but that dress just about clings on her body type of dress - check.

Why didn't Roxy tell me that Caitlin was coming?

I do a double take to make sure it's her, and it sure is —Caitlin O'Halloran, my best friend's sister and the girl next door. Porcelain skin that's earned her more than her fair share of offers from acting and modeling scouts when she was in high school and that dazzling smile that I know so well. Too bad she's flashing her pearly whites at the last man I'd expected to see her with, Malcolm Carter, top senior analyst and resident company asshole. He's also the same guy who framed the article that named both of us among the top twenty top analysts in the country and makes sure everyone in the company knows it.

My jaw clenches as Malcolm's hand lowers down to the curve of Caitlin's back. Questions race through my mind: How long have they known each other? How did they meet? Social media? Her brother? No, can't be her brother. Jordan wouldn't be able to stand the guy. Must be her friend, Roxy.

I watch as Malcolm introduces Caitlin to the guys he hangs out with, the same guys he boasts about every woman he sleeps with, each 'lay' lauded with a nickname I can't even imagine pinned on my best friend's sister.

As her eyes scan the room, Caitlin sees me and with an excited exclamation, is in my arms, the smell of her shampoo filling my senses. Within seconds, I'm transported to her mother's kitchen where Jordan and I chow down on freshly baked cookies and then riding our bikes to the park where we'd play ball with the other kids. How long has it been since I'd last seen her? Eight months? A year? I'd been in Saint Lucia the last time she returned home.

"Campbell, I can't believe you're here!" she exclaims as I let her down. Just a few inches shorter than my 6'2" frame, she should be a model but she chooses to bury her nose researching about genes and disease. "Did you get my texts?"

I stare at her, the realization that I hadn't responded to her texts hitting me. I'd told myself I'd get to them later. And now, it's later. "Crap. I did but I forgot to reply. Sorry, Cait."

She shrugs. "That's okay because this is the best Christmas present ever. You're here!"

Behind her, Malcolm clears his throat. "Small world. How do you two know each other?"

"She's my buddy's sister," I reply. "So you better be nice, man." There's an edge in my voice that I hadn't intended to come out but I can't help it. He better not give her a nickname like he's done to every woman he's bragged to the other guys about.

Caitlin grabs my arm. "Yup, he sure is. Campbell grew up next door and I've known him forever."

"So how do you guys know each other?" I ask.

"*Roxy*," they both answer in unison, and as they laugh at their timing, it all makes sense. Roxy's all about matchmaking her friends even if her attempts, like this one, don't make any sense. Why the hell would she match Caitlin with Malcolm, of all people?

"So you two are going out for the first time tonight?" I ask and Caitlin nods.

"Babe, why don't we join the rest of the guys and have some fun? The night is young and they don't call this the hottest place in Manhattan to party for nothing," Malcolm says, his hand drifting down the small of her back.

Before I can say goodbye, Malcolm whisks Caitlin

away and I watch them disappear into the crowd. Great. Now there's no way I'm heading home knowing she's with him. Hell no. I've always been protective of Caitlin whenever her older brother isn't around and knowing the guys at my office, I can't help but feel even more protective than I already do. Besides, if Jordan knew of Malcolm's reputation, I'm sure he'd do the same thing.

But as Mitch and the other guys from my department beckon for me to join them by the window, I remind myself that Caitlin's no longer in junior high. She's old enough to do whatever she wants, even if it's being asshole Malcolm Carter's holiday party date.

Two hours later, I'm pretty much done partying. I've drunk my fill of watered-down gin and tonic, danced, tried not to talk business with the other employees, and as I stand next to the window watching the forecasted rain fall on the city, I'm finally ready to go home. Caitlin's date seems to be going well and I'm happy for her although I'm worried about all the drinks she's having. She's probably had three drinks already. Tall sweet ones that are guaranteed to pack a punch. But the same old reminder I've been telling myself crops up: Cait's old enough to take care of herself and I sure as hell am not here as her babysitter.

As I turn away from the window, the kiss—more like the bumping of lips—that comes catches me by surprise. It's soft and warm and immediately followed by a familiar giggle.

"Oops! Sorry," Caitlin exclaims as I reach around her waist to hold her up. "Fancy meeting you here, stranger." The way she says stranger is funny, like *strange* and *her* blended into one long word. But of course, it is. Caitlin O'Halloran is officially drunk.

"Where's Malcolm?"

She cocks her head toward the crowd. "He's somewhere. I bailed out on him."

"Why? What happened?"

Caitlin doesn't answer right away. She gazes at my red tie before running her fingers down the length of it, stopping just along my sternum. "This suits you perfectly, you know, this tie. I never realized how sexy you look wearing a suit. Whenever I see you, you're always wearing casual stuff."

"That's because I'm not working whenever I see you."

"Oh, so you're working tonight? I thought you were partying."

"I am now," I reply. "Anyway, what happened to Malcolm?"

She turns serious, an exaggerated pout giving her a childish expression.

"I went to ladies room and when I returned, he was making out with some girl right on the dance floor. Then he pretended not to see me," she pauses, as if trying to remember something. "But wait. Let me preface that. He kept trying to kiss me and I wasn't having any of that nonsense, not even if I'm roaring drunk."

That's my girl, I almost say out loud but I don't, not when I want to beat the crap out of Malcolm first.

"I mean, hello?" she continues. "It's our first date! I mean, come on! And what's up with his hand on my ass all damn night?"

"Hell, no, he didn't." I take a step away from the window. Now I really need to beat the shit out of him.

Caitlin grabs my arm. "It's okay, Cam. I took care of it and shut that crap down right away. I can take of myself."

I look at her, her words reminding me that she's right. She can take care of herself. She's all grown up. "Someone still needs to beat the crap out of him."

"Well, it's not going to be you," she says. "Look, Cam, I just need to go home."

"How many drinks did you have, Cait?"

She thinks for a few moments, her brow furrowing. "I had sex with the bartender twice. Or was it three times?"

"You had what?!"

She laughs. "I knew I'd get you. Don't worry. It's a

drink Roxy made for me, called Sex with the Bartender."

"How many drinks did you have exactly?"

She holds up three fingers. Actually she can't seem to know how many fingers she's holding up. First, it's two fingers, then three. Whether she's had two or three drinks, that's still a lot of rum for a girl who doesn't drink much. "Oh, and Malcolm did order me two other drinks. Or was it one?"

"Wow, Cait, that's a lot."

"Anyway, I'm leaving," she announces as I follow her to the elevator and she starts punching the buttons until she hits the one for the lobby. "I need to go home."

"I'll take you home."

"You don't have to, Cam. You're not my babysitter."

"I know, but it's also two in the morning."

"It is?" She looks at me incredulously as the elevator doors open and she steps inside.

"And there's also no way I'm letting you get in a cab by yourself."

"You're not my knight in shining armor, Campbell Murphy. Not tonight."

"No, I'm not. But that doesn't the change the fact that as your brother's friend, I always keep an eye on you when he's not around to do so."

We don't talk the rest of the way to the lobby. I help her with her coat and walk her just before the front lobby doors. Outside, it's raining, the streets glistening.

"I'll be fine, Cam. Besides, I don't want you taking me all the way home and then having to drive back to the city. I mean, you live only a few blocks from here. Midtown, right?"

"Why don't you stay over at my place for the night and I'll drive you home in the morning? How does that sound?"

"What about your girlfriend?"

"I'm not seeing anyone right now," I say. "Besides, even if I did have a girlfriend, it wouldn't change a thing. You're my best friend's sister and I'm taking care of you. Come on," I take her hand and lead her out the front doors just as a cab stops in front of us.

Perfect timing.

"I'm so glad you're here, Cam," Caitlin says as she slides into the back seat and I follow right after her. I give the driver my address and we sit in silence, gazing out the window as the rain starts to come down in sheets. "We just missed that, didn't we? So much for my idea to go home."

I study her, amused when she flinches as thunder rumbles overhead followed by lightning streaking across the sky. Her green eyes look upward in awe. "You're not used to the rain anymore, are you?"

"I've been living in California for the last three

years, Cam. It hardly rains, which means there's no thunder or lightning either."

I pull her to me and feel her rest her head on my shoulder. I kiss the top of her head. "I'll hold you through it all. Don't worry."

She giggles. "Thank you, my knight in shining armor."

Ten minutes later, we arrive at my apartment building, walking past the doorman toward the elevator. It's an older building but well-maintained. It's also just as expensive as every other building simply because it's in Midtown Manhattan.

I unlock the door to my one-bedroom high-rise apartment and we step inside. As Caitlin shrugs off her coat and hands it to me, she stares at the sight beyond the full-length window at the other end of the apartment. "Wow! Jory wasn't kidding when he said you could see the Empire State Building from your living room."

"He and your dad helped renovate this place so he should know." As Caitlin slips off her boots and heads for the window, I remember how the view was the only saving grace about the apartment when I first bought it four years ago. Fresh out of Harvard, I was young, bright-eyed, and deep in student loan debt. So why not incur more debt by living in the city? At least, the renovation didn't cost me too much. All Mr. O'Halloran wanted was my enthusiastic referral of O'Halloran Builders to colleagues and friends.

Three years later and thanks to the hefty bonuses I've made with every deal we've closed, all my student loan debt is all paid off. But no matter the cost associated with living in the city, this apartment was also one of the best decisions I've ever made. It had me living close to the financial heart of the city where I was determined to make my mark. It's also a place all my own, which means I'll never find myself at the mercy of someone else again.

Sitting on the couch, Caitlin pulls out her phone from her purse and dials a number. "I'm letting Mom and Dad know where I am before they freak out. They're at a party in New Jersey but they should be home by now."

I join Caitlin on the couch and listen to her leave a message to her parents telling them she's with me and that she'll be home the next day. After she hangs up the phone and sets it on the coffee table, we watch the lights at the top of the Empire State Building change colors for a few minutes until I catch her yawning.

"Why don't we get you to bed? It's late."

"Can I sleep here?"

I shake my head. "No. You take the bed."

"But–"

I get up from the couch and extend my hand toward her. Caitlin sighs and takes my hand. "Oh, alright."

"I'll set out an extra toothbrush and a towel for you in the bathroom. And you can use my shirt for bed if you want."

She follows me to the bedroom. "I'm sorry for crashing here tonight, Cam."

"Don't be. I'm glad you're here, to be honest." Better with me than with Malcolm, that's for sure. I pull down the covers on the bed. "You take the bed and I'll take the couch."

"Cam, I can't do that–"

"No arguing," I say, a fake stern look on my face as I open my dresser and take out a pajama set courtesy of her parents last Christmas, neatly folded and never used, and hand it to her. "The bathroom's over there and I'll see you in the morning."

I grab a shirt and a pair of sweatpants for myself and step outside. I can't help but feel relieved that Malcolm couldn't help being what he was, a jerk who made a move on another woman while on a date with someone else. But that's his problem. I can't believe how much better I feel knowing Caitlin's safe with me.

She may be old enough to take care of herself but she's still Jordan's sister.

THREE

Caitlin

My headache wakes me up first—that and the smell of coffee wafting from the kitchen. As I force myself to sit up on the bed, there's a knock on the door and Campbell sticks his head in.

"I could hear you groaning all the way from the kitchen," he says. "How's your hangover?"

"Do you have to ask?"

He shrugs. "Care for some coffee?"

"Can I brush my teeth first?"

"That would be a good idea, Cait. Sure."

I rush to the bathroom, hating that my hair is a mess and I must look a fright. But at least, I should get an A for effort. A girl's got to look presentable first thing in the morning especially in the presence of a boy, even if he's just her brother's best friend. I'm sure Campbell has seen me in worse shape when we were kids. Problem is, we're not kids anymore and I have to admit, he's a lot more built than the last time I remember seeing him. When did he fill out? When did his biceps get so hard and toned? Even his jaw has gotten wider only because his neck is wider, too. Has he been working out?

When I return to the bedroom five minutes later, Campbell is standing by the window. He drew open the shades while I was inside the bathroom and I cover my eyes as I stumble back to the bed. Outside, the clouds are still gray and thick but it's not raining.

"Why do I suddenly feel like I just crawled out of my coffin when I shouldn't have?"

"Because you're hung over." He hands me a pair of sunglasses. "Here. Put those on and I'll get the coffee."

I prop the thick pillows against the headboard and lean back, gazing at the flannel pajamas I'm wearing. This one has cute Dalmatian puppies running all over it.

"Are these from my parents?"

"Yup, from last year. It's become a tradition, I've noticed." He hands me a mug of coffee.

"It's probably because that's how they remember you every Christmas morning, knocking on our door to see what Santa got us for Christmas… and you, since Santa left you presents, too. Do you remember that?"

Campbell nods. "Of course, I remember. But we're grown up now and I don't wear PJ's anymore."

"What do you wear to bed?"

He shrugs. "Nothing."

I feel my cheeks redden and remind myself to sip my coffee, the vision of a naked Campbell who's all grown up under the covers making my lady bits tingle. They shouldn't, especially since he's my brother's best friend and up until this morning, I've never even entertained the thought.

"You never know," I say, switching the subject back. "Old habits die hard. They just might get you another set again. Besides, I miss those days when we were still kids and we didn't have a single care in the world."

Campbell doesn't say anything and it hits me. While Jordan and I didn't have to worry about anything when we were kids, it was different for him. Campbell used to tell us that his best memories came from his interactions with our family and the two years he lived with us after his mom had to sell their house to pay off her husband's debts. Mr. Murphy had taken a loan on the house without telling her; he even forged her signature. I'm sure it went to his second family, the one he ran off with when he abandoned Campbell and his mother.

I clear my throat. "You still plan on staying the night, right? We're changing it up a bit since Addison and Jordan will be celebrating Christmas Day with her parents, and so Christmas Day dinner will be on Christmas Eve."

He sips his coffee. "Of course. I wouldn't miss it for the world."

I pat the space next to me. "Sit with me, Cam. It's your bed, remember?"

He sits next to me and for the next few minutes, we don't talk. We're just two people enjoying a good cup of coffee. I sigh happily, feeling my headache receding with each sip. "You make good coffee."

"French press."

"I do instant mostly because I need instant gratification"

Campbell stares at me in mock horror. "Do I even know you? Instant coffee is not real coffee."

"Yes, it is."

"No, it isn't."

"Yes, it is."

We laugh, back to the same back and forth bantering we've always done since we were kids. It used to drive my parents crazy while Jordan would just roll his eyes before telling us to quit it. We become quiet again, our attention back on enjoying our coffee.

"I was really drunk last night, wasn't I?" I say quietly. "I hope I didn't make a fool of myself."

Campbell pats my hand resting on the covers between us. "No, you didn't. You were just fine. You conked out actually."

I pout. "You're just saying that to make me feel better."

"You don't remember throwing up, do you? I didn't have to hold your hair away from your face as you threw up in the toilet?" Campbell asks and I shake my head, horrified by the visual his words presented. "Then you were fine. You were just a wee bit drunk." He holds his thumb and index finger two inches away as I chuckle.

"Thanks for making me feel better. I do feel like shit though."

"Three drinks will do that to you, Cait, especially if you're a lightweight," he says as I glare at him even though I know he's right.

We don't talk for the next few minutes again, either too busy enjoying our coffee or probably wondering what to say next. I look around his bedroom, its simple masculine design evident in the heather gray tones of the walls that match the dark gray of the bed covers and the headboard. A large painting hangs overhead. There's a floating bookcase on one wall filled with architecture and travel books opposite the window that's covered with floor-to-ceiling wide horizontal blinds. A lone modern chair sits in one corner next to the door leading to the walk-in closet.

"One thing about you, Cam, is that you're such a perfectionist that even your bedroom is perfect," I say.

"Come to think of it, your whole apartment is perfect. You even have a view of the Empire State Building."

Campbell chuckles. "That's what everyone usually remembers."

"You used to be this neat when you lived with us, too. Remember?" I nudge his shoulder with my elbow. "You had strict rules of me not entering it at all."

He rolls his eyes. "That's because you used to come in and make a huge mess of everything."

I make a face. "Oh, that's right. I was a pest, wasn't I?" Actually, now that I remember things through the fog of my hangover, I was more than a pest. When I was eight and he was twelve or thirteen, I told my parents I was going to marry Campbell Murphy.

"Nah, you were alright." He finishes his coffee. "Anyway, when I first bought this place it had so many dividing walls and closets that it looked even smaller than it really was. I knew I had to do something to get the spaciousness you see now. I remember your dad giving me the sledgehammer so I could break one of the walls down."

I smile, visualizing him with the sledgehammer. Imagining my brother and my dad doing it is easy but Campbell? "And now you've got an amazing place. It's so... so you. Simple yet classic. A bachelor's pad! That's what it is."

I don't know why I'm blabbering but somehow, his

apartment is just the epitome of him as a person. Simple and classic. Trustworthy. Smart. Neat. Gorgeous as he sits next to me in his t-shirt and sweatpants.

A bachelor.

"Why, thanks, Cait. Are you sure you're not still drunk?" I can almost swear I see a blush creep on his cheeks as he smiles. "But I can't claim all the credit. Jordan and your dad helped with the design and the build out. You should have seen this when I bought it. It was so outdated. Your dad figured it would do well as a test renovation project for his company's portfolio and I was all for it."

"How come I don't remember that going on?"

"Because you were buried in college papers," he says, touching the tip of my nose with his index finger. "Anyway, O'Halloran Builders did an amazing job with this place."

"It suits you, Cam."

"Thanks."

"Anyway, maybe I should call Roxy and tell her what a dud Malcolm turned out to be. I should have her set me up with someone new. Knowing her, she won't give up until she finds the right match for me."

The silence that follows makes me wonder if Campbell heard me but I don't push it. I must have been embarrassing last night given how many drinks I'd had.

"You done with your coffee?" he asks, getting up from the bed and I nod. "Let me take it to the kitchen."

"Did I say something wrong?" I ask as he stops by the door and shakes his head.

"No, but you're right. Maybe Roxy can find you a better match next time. She seems to enjoy playing matchmaker anyway. I think Jordan's mother-in-law is into the same thing, too. She's determined to find a match for me one of these days."

I follow Campbell out of the bedroom, hating that our time together is over too soon. I enjoy being around him. I can be myself and not worry about watching what I say even if sometimes I say the silliest things. But I also know that I can't remain his Jordan's annoying baby sister all the time. We all have to grow up somehow and maybe even move on.

As I walk into the living room, I stop and look around. The rest of his apartment is as perfect as the bedroom, in varied tones of white with gray accent walls, an electric fireplace situated close to the tall windows with their gorgeous view of the city. But as perfect as everything looks, something is missing. "Where's your tree?"

"What tree?"

"Your Christmas tree."

He shrugs. "I don't need one."

"What do you mean you don't need one? It's Christmas, Campbell Murphy."

"I know it is, but I usually spend it with your family anyway, so I don't need one."

"But what happens when you come home?" I ask, pointing to a spot in front of the couch. "It's empty."

He shrugs again, rinsing the mugs and stacking them in the dishwasher. "I sleep. I work. I hang out with friends. And when I come home, I play my video games. Besides, there are Christmas trees everywhere I go. It's no big deal, Cait. It's just Christmas."

As I look at Campbell, I can't believe I never saw it before, the quiet boy who became the man of the house when his father abandoned him and his mother for another woman. Mr. Murphy even bailed out on child support payments the first few months by fleeing to France, forcing Campbell's mother to sell their house just to pay the debts he left behind. When she found a live-in job as a cook for a wealthy family in the Hamptons, my parents suggested that Campbell live with us for two years until he graduated high school. That way he didn't have to transfer schools where his mother wouldn't have been around to take care of him anyway.

Campbell worked hard those two years when he lived with us, earning straight A's and eventually landing a scholarship at an Ivy League university. His mother moved to Miami and lives her own life with her new husband while his father, as far as I know, is still pretty much persona non grata. At least, that's what Jordan told me once before telling me not to mention Mr. Murphy around Campbell again. Still, this whole 'it's just Christmas' crap is ridiculous and I'm not buying it. Not one bit.

"What do you mean, *it's just Christmas?* It's not just Christmas, Cam. It's Christmas!" I emphasize that last word in case he didn't hear me the first time. "We have to get you a tree. Like, we have to."

He laughs. "No, we're not. I don't have room for one."

"Yes, we are, and yes, you do have room. We'll *find* room. So what are your plans for the day?"

"I was going to drop you off and check out the Union Square Holiday Market."

I clap my hands. "Oh my gosh! Can I come? I need to shop for Jordan and Addy and Piper and it's my goal not to order anything online this year. I want to support local arts and crafts. Can I? Can I? Can I?"

Campbell looks at me for a few seconds, amused, before he bursts out laughing. But he doesn't say yes or no.

"Can I?" This time I flash him my best sad puppy dog impression. "Please? While we're at it, we can even shop for the ornaments that will go on your future tree."

I even bat my eyelashes.

"Okay then." He laughs as I wrap my arms around him in a hug. I feel his arms tighten around my waist, his hard chest pressing against my breasts as a tingle travels down my belly. I step away, surprised.

"What?" he asks as I shake my head.

"Nothing."

His brow furrows as he studies my face, then he shrugs. "Let me get you a towel so you can shower and get ready. I'll go in after you're done."

Half an hour later, I step out of the bathroom wearing Campbell's robe. It has that clean soap smell that I like so much. I bury my nose in the plush collar and take a deep breath. I can smell him, too, and it's nice.

"Hey, I'm done in the bathroom," I announce as he gets up from the couch, the laptop perched on the coffee table. "Wait! Are you working? Isn't it the weekend?"

"Just sending emails." He closes the laptop and heads into the bathroom, leaving the door partially open. Soon, I hear the shower running.

I can't explain it but I've always felt safe around Campbell. Maybe it's because he's my brother's best friend and my unofficial 'other' brother. I can be myself around him, not worried about being too smart for my own good. I can be weird and nerdy, too, and he totally gets it only because he's just as nerdy. He used to program video games in middle school and for a while, we all thought he'd find a job with some gaming company but he ended up working in finance instead.

I slip on the dress I wore the night before, glad I'd picked one that wasn't too short. With the forecast calling for rain last night, there was no way I was wearing something too short or stilettos for that matter. Instead, I'd worn knee-high boots with my dress which work out perfect for today's excursion to the holiday market.

Satisfied with the way I look, I step out of the bedroom and head toward the living room. But I stop when I see him through the gap in the door.

Wearing only a towel around his hips and his back toward me, Campbell is standing in front of the mirror brushing his teeth. I stare. Forget the nerd. Since when did he get all bulked up?

I can see the muscles on his shoulders and back ripple with every movement, the unmistakable indentation of one muscle to the next tightening. Even his buttocks look perfect from under the towel. When he runs his fingers through his dark hair, I can't help but stare at his back and the way his broad shoulders taper to slim hips. Goodness gracious, but the sight of Campbell Murphy all grown up is enough to chase even the worst hangover away. When my gaze moves upward on the mirror, our eyes meet and he winks at me.

"Oh! Sorry!" I mumble, walking away. I head to the kitchen to get a drink of water, needing something to distract me. I down the full glass of water in one gulp, blowing out a breath as I stare at the blank spot next to the electric fireplace. But all I can think of is Campbell naked, no towel this time.

What if he'd turned around?

I shake the dirty thoughts of Campbell out of my head. He's my brother's best friend, for crying out loud, and I have no business thinking he's anything but that. It's exactly the reason why I feel so comfortable around him, because I trust him just as much as Jordan trusts him, too. Even my parents trust him.

Doing anything with him outside the realm of friendship can never be on the agenda at all. Well, unless we get stuck on a deserted island somewhere and we get bored. But there's only one problem: we're not on a deserted island. And I'm definitely not bored.

"Hey, you ready?"

Campbell's voice snaps me out of my thoughts and I nod, pointing to the empty space in front of me. "I was just thinking the tree would look good over here. Maybe a Fraser Fir only because they're the best in my opinion. Maybe five or six feet tall? What do you think?"

Campbell is wearing black jeans and a light blue

shirt that plays off his blue eyes. His hair is still slightly damp and an errant curl has made its way to the middle of his forehead. "I think you're right. I'm actually glad you brought it up. You always had the best ideas, Cait."

More like insist on it, I almost add although I'm glad he's being a good sport about it. He could easily have said no. But I'm blushing and I hate it because it's as if I've suddenly lost control of my body. There are butterflies fluttering about in my belly, too.

"Oh, gosh, Cam. Thanks!" I giggle only to feel the pounding inside my head resume. "Ouch!"

"You're welcome." He takes my coat from the rack in the hallway, cocking his head toward the door. "Care to have breakfast first? That should help with your hangover."

FOUR

Campbell

I never planned on getting a Christmas tree, not when I spend every Christmas with the O'Halloran's and their tree is amazing, covered with everything from Jordan's paper chain from first grade to Caitlin's glued-up stick manger from fourth grade, every single ornament carefully stored in their attic. There are even a few of my own creations, like a hardened clay reindeer and one that looks like the Empire State Building missing its antenna.

Their tree is also lit up with enough lights that it could be mistaken for a beacon by intelligent life in outer space. But I don't care. It's a tradition for the O'Halloran family, one that I look forward to every year, and when I get to start my own family, I'm going to do the exact same thing.

That way, I get to honor them for everything they've

done for me, treating me like I'd always been part of their family. I even have my very own stocking hanging from the mantel that Mrs. O as I call Mrs. O'Halloran sewed for me when I was twelve.

That was when my parents' problems began, when Dad didn't come home some nights, claiming he was traveling. Only he wasn't. He'd started seeing someone he met at work and eventually lived with her, balancing his life between our house and hers all under the guise of traveling for work until he couldn't do it anymore. When I turned sixteen, he left Mom a note saying he'd found someone else and that they were moving to France where she had family and property. We'd find out later that he had two daughters with her, my half-sisters although I've never met them.

There were no other goodbyes other than that stupid note he wrote for Mom. He couldn't even be bothered to write me one. For the next four months, Mom had to scramble to make ends meet because he was always late with his child support payments that we eventually had to sell the house when the creditors came calling.

That's when I moved in with the O'Halloran's while Mom found a live-in job as a house manager in the Hamptons. It would prove to be two of the best years of my life. It was pure chaos in the O'Halloran household but it was a good chaos—a happy one. Sure, Jordan often got into trouble and Caitlin would stay past curfew, but it wasn't anything major. Certainly nothing like my dad abandoning his family to run off with his mistress.

But I tell myself to stop thinking about the past, not when my present looks darn good in the form of my buddy's sister sitting across from me and talking my ear off about her latest dissertation, something about dopamine levels and Alzheimer's disease.

I try to keep up the best I can, relieved that I don't have to consult my phone to know that dopamine is a feel-good hormone and that Alzheimer's disease is a condition characterized by mental decline and dementia. Caitlin is animated as she speaks, her hands moving in front of her, slender fingers gracefully illustrating one point and then another. And then there's her laughter, light and happy.

So Caitlin.

"Are you going to stay there after graduation?" I ask when she finishes talking to take a bite out of her omelet. We're at one of my favorite places to hang out, a small cafe a few blocks from my apartment that's known for their crepes.

"I don't know yet. I received an offer from the university hospital but I was hoping to get one closer to home."

"That would be wonderful if you could work here, wouldn't it?"

Caitlin nods, her eyes sparkling. "Yes, it would. Then I'd be close to everyone again. That means I can bug you more than I already do."

"You can bug me anytime, Cait," I say, grinning. "I thought you already knew that."

We finish our breakfast half an hour later and make our way to the Union Square Holiday Market, a European-style winter market known for its unique gifts by local craftsman and artists.

Barely noon, the holiday market is already filled with New Yorkers doing last-minute shopping like us. It's where I usually find gifts for the O'Halloran family, from hand-painted silk scarves and fair trade wool socks for Mr. and Mrs. O to board games for Jordan and felted owls for Caitlin who used to be crazy about owls for years although I'm not sure if she is anymore.

"I can't believe it's been years since I've been here. It's even better than the last time I remember it." She grabs my hand, leading me toward a booth selling art drawn on old book pages. "We're definitely going to need more than two pairs of hands to carry everything back!"

Even without makeup, Caitlin looks amazing, her red dress peeking from underneath her black wool coat. She's always been a stunning beauty, words I'd never say out loud in front of her brother. With her flaming red hair, porcelain skin and dazzling smile, she's a sight for sore eyes and always finds a way to make me smile.

I remember my simmering anger at my father when I first moved into the spare bedroom in the O'Halloran home, not knowing who to blame for his decision to leave us. While Jordan's solution was to get me out of the house and keep me busy with sports, Caitlin filled the silence with her drawings that she'd stick to my walls, usually owls in all shapes, colors, and sizes. While she may have been too young then to know what it felt like to be abandoned, I never forgot her little gestures of friendship.

We stop by a booth selling personalized Christmas decorations and Caitlin finds one that's stamped with the year and the words, *Campbell's First Christmas*.

"I think I'll add 'tree' here," she says, pointing to the space under the word, Christmas. "That way, it's going to mark the first time you put up your very first Christmas tree. What do you think?"

"I think it's a wonderful idea."

"Awesome! We're going to have a wonderful time, Cam! I just know it."

I'd long given up arguing with Caitlin about having a tree at my apartment only because she's right. I have to have a tree, at least, even if it's just for this year, and I have a feeling that this one will just be overloaded with so many decorations it probably will fall over from the weight.

After half an hour of walking around and surveying what's on sale, we set out to tackle our list. The first on my list is Piper, my god daughter who also happens to be Caitlin's as well. I didn't even have to think twice about it when Jordan asked me. It was an automatic yes even if I had to take a series of classes about my responsibilities as Piper's godfather. I've even done my share of babysitting, the usual game controllers we used to hold on to from the days when Jordan and I used to hang out have now been replaced with baby bottles and teething toys.

"What do you think of this?" I hold up a crocheted doll with hair made of reddish orange yarn. "There are no buttons for her eyes and nothing that's bound to come loose. And it's a redhead. It should be safe for a baby, right?"

"That's the cutest thing, Cam! And perfect! I think it goes perfectly with this one." She picks up another doll from the basket and holds it up. It's a crocheted boy doll with black yarn for hair although you only see the ends as it peeks out of a patterned beanie.

I hold the girl doll next to the one she's holding. "They're a perfect pair."

"Just like the two of you," says the woman behind the counter. "You guys look so cute together."

"Oh, we're not dating." Caitlin says at the same time I mutter that we're just friends.

"I'm sorry if I put you two on the spot," the young woman says, grinning. "Doesn't mean you guys don't look cute together though."

I clear my throat. "Did you make these or are they imported from somewhere?"

"Oh no, I made all the dolls in the booth!" she says, laughing. "I have an online store and I usually sell patterns but I like making them for the holidays and as special orders." She points to her business cards next to some of the smaller dolls. I take a card and slip it into my coat pocket.

"Are you getting that one?" Caitlin points to the doll I'm still holding. "I think she'd be perfect for Piper."

"Yes, I am. I want to get her some baby clothes, too."

"Oh, and let's not forget one of those Baby's First Christmas ornaments," Caitlin adds as I hand both dolls to the woman behind the counter and pay for them. Somehow, I don't want the doll I picked out to be lonely, not when Caitlin picked the perfect match for it complete with the crocheted beanie.

Two hours later, we make it back to my apartment, arms laden with bags filled with tree ornaments and presents for everyone on our list except each other—unless Caitlin managed to find something for me when I wasn't looking. In the past, she's given me a tie clip, a pair of cufflinks, and an old poetry book she found at an estate sale in LA. This year, I guess it's the idea of a real Christmas tree inside my apartment and that personalized ornament.

Then it's a trek back down so we can find the perfect tree at the tree lot three blocks away. Caitlin is relentless but I'm not complaining. It's the first day of my holiday vacation and I have nothing else planned anyway. I haven't even thought about work at all, no financial models to make, no reports to check.

At the lot, we're mistaken for a couple shopping for our first tree together but I let it slide. So does Caitlin—or maybe she didn't hear the attendant. And maybe it's just easier that way. No need to explain that there's no way we're together for she's totally off-limits. But why do I feel a tug in my chest every time I look at her?

We settle for a five-foot Fraser Fir and although the attendant promises to deliver it within the hour, Caitlin insists we can both carry it home with her holding one end and me holding the other. And we do. She's that determined to get a proper Christmas tree in my apartment and I'm glad at least one of us is that determined.

Once inside, we set out to decorate the tree and by the time we're done two hours later, the living room is a mess of wrappers, ribbons, and tinsel. I'm exhausted but even I have to admit that the tree looks great against the backdrop of the city with the Empire State Building in the distance. Caitlin even found an online station that played holiday songs the entire time and I didn't mind it one bit.

On the drive home, we hardly talk. Maybe she's tired from all the things we did during the day or maybe we just ran out of things to say. But I can sense something else. It reminds me of the low that follows after an intense high, when you're having so much fun but life happens and you have to come back down. Maybe that's what's going on... or maybe not.

"I really had a wonderful time today, Cam. Thanks for rescuing me last night," she says as I make a right from Queens Boulevard toward Forest Hills.

"You're welcome."

"And thanks for putting up with me today," she adds. "Sometimes I forget that you need your space, too."

"Don't say that, Cait. If I felt I had to put up with you, I would have told you," I say. "Actually I had a lot of fun today. If you weren't there, I'd have gone to the gym, checked my email and that would have been the end of that. I probably would have ended up working."

She grins. "I know, but just in case."

"Cait, it's really no big deal," I say. "Probably my only complaint would be having Roxy pick a better date for you next time. If you decide to go for a second try."

She laughs, pulling out her phone and glancing at

the display. "Yeah, she's been dying to find out what happened so I guess she doesn't know that Malcolm bailed out on me."

"Maybe you can let her know your preferences or something," I add, parking the car in front of their house. "Maybe she'll find you a better match that way. What type of guy do you normally like?"

Caitlin thinks for a few moments as I park the car in their driveway. "I don't know. I like them to be smart and funny, I guess."

I chuckle. "You've got to be more specific than that. Serial killers can be smart and funny, too."

She gives a half shrug. "I guess someone I can be myself with."

"That's it?"

"Does tall, dark, and handsome with six-pack abs count? Someone who can make me laugh and tell me things I don't know and yet still be interesting. Someone who can cook because I sure can't cook even if my life depends on it, and someone who won't mind it if I'm not as tidy as most women."

"Now that last one could be a deal breaker for most guys," I say as she glares at me. "Just kidding."

"Someone who is classy and knows how to have fun."

"That's a good list of qualities to start with, Cait," I

say. "You should tell Roxy that. Maybe she can find someone who fits those qualifications."

She peers at me curiously. "You do know I was just kidding about the second chance at matchmaking, right? Because I sure as heck don't have any time to date anyone."

"Why not?"

"Because I just want to graduate and get a job first," she replies. "That means I need to focus on getting a job instead of playing around with some guy."

"How does that saying go? All work and no play makes Caitlin a dull girl."

"So? I don't mind being dull. Better be dull and rich than pretty and poor. Although I'm far from rich until I get a decent job." She reaches for the door handle but I stop her, grabbing her wrist that's closest to me.

"Hey, where'd that come from? You never used to worry about money and all that."

"I don't know, Cam. I guess it's just seeing everyone around me making it. They have their own apartments, their own jobs. No need for an allowance from Mom and Dad... that kind of thing," she says. "Look at you."

"What about me?"

"You've got your own apartment and it's in Manhattan. Look at Addison–"

"Addison is not you, Cait. She's also older than you by what? Seven years?" I say. "Most of my reasons for having my own place in the city has to do with work. Some are selfish, others are more personal reasons that I'm not willing to share with anyone. But other than that, such things don't come without a price."

"I don't know, Cam. I guess at twenty-five, I feel that I shouldn't be a student forever even if I am working toward my Masters. I guess it's just hitting me, that's all. Seeing everyone at the party last night so successful and talking about their bonuses which I can only dream about. Malcolm said his bonus was a hundred grand. Who gets a hundred grand?"

People like me who don't have time to put up a tree because it'll only remind them of an empty apartment, I almost tell her. "I'm sorry Malcolm had to brag about his bonus," I say instead. "He's a dick and honestly, Cait, I'm so glad you ended up with me last night."

She smiles. "I am, too. It was meant to be, I guess."

"Yes, it was."

She squeezes my hand. "Anyway, thanks for the ride home. You don't have to walk me to the door, by the way."

"The hell I'm not." I push my door open and step outside. "I'll carry these inside for you."

She grabs her coat from her lap as I open the door for her. "I just figured it would save you time, that's all."

I don't say anything as she steps out of the SUV. Grabbing the shopping bags from the back seat, I follow her to the front door. I can almost feel my happiness from the day go down with each step, like a tank running out of gas. But as she slips the keys into the lock, I also know it's not exactly that. Why does it feel like the end of an amazing date even though we weren't exactly on a date?

"Hey, Cait?"

She whips around to face me. "Yeah?"

"I've got tickets to *Coriolanus* two nights from now and I was wondering if you'd like to come with me."

"*Coriolanus*? As in the hottest ticket in town *Coriolanus*? The one with Ashe Hunter, the British actor?"

I nod. "Yeah. That *Coriolanus*. My boss can't make it so he gave it to me last night before he left the party."

Caitlin peers at me suspiciously. "And you haven't asked anyone else to go with you yet?"

"No, but I'm asking you, silly," I reply, laughing. "You wanna come with me or should I call someone–"

"Are you kidding? Of course I want to go! I'm not about to say no to Coriolanus."

"That's good then. Maybe we can have a few drinks before we go."

She nods. "Sure."

"Does six work for you?"

Her eyes narrow. "This isn't like a date, is it? I mean, just to be sure. You're not asking me out on a date."

A lump forms in my throat. I never really thought

about it that way but if she'd rather not see it as a date, then fine. "Not if don't want me to. We can call it a no-date date, if that makes you feel better."

"That sounds... corny. But for now, it works. No-date date it is then." She turns away from me to push the door open and step inside. As I set the shopping bags on the floor, I can't help but grin when I see the Christmas tree in the far corner, the space underneath it spilling over with presents, most of them with pink ribbons, and I'm willing to bet they're likely Piper's, the first O'Halloran grandchild. I inhale, taking in the scents of the home I once lived in for two years.

Suddenly memories come rushing in, of Christmas morning when the three of us would rush downstairs to open our presents and we'd show off what we got while Mr. and Mrs. O'Halloran laughed at our exuberance. We were no longer kids then—Jordan and I seniors in high school while Caitlin was in middle school—but it didn't matter. Caitlin and I used to be in charge of preparing traditional hot chocolate together, complete with semi-sweet chocolate and whipped cream. There was no judgment in the O'Halloran home.

"Hey, you okay?" Caitlin's voice breaks through my reverie and I nod.

"Yeah, I'm just amazed at your parents' tree. It's like a Hallmark movie come to life."

"I didn't know you watched Hallmark movies,

Campbell."

"I don't but one of my ex-girlfriends did," I reply. "She cried over everything."

"Oh." Caitlin bites her lower lip, looking down at the floor. "So, are you seeing anyone right now?"

I pick up the day's mail that's sitting on the floor next to the door and hand it to her. "Nah."

"Not even dating?"

"Not seriously."

"So, casual dating then?" She sets the mail on top of the console.

"Maybe. Maybe not. Why do you ask?"

"Nothing," Caitlin replies quickly, busying herself with the mail before setting it back down.

"Well, I better get going." I turn back toward the door. "I'll see you on Thursday at six?"

"Yup, Thursday at six."

I do my best to walk down to my car without looking behind me but I can't help myself. When I do, I catch Caitlin outside the front door watching me. She lifts her hand in a subtle wave as I get behind the wheel and start the Range Rover, doing my best to act cool. I don't even know why I have to work hard at looking cool but somehow, I do.

Don't look back, man. Don't look back.

But I look anyway, this time through my rearview mirror as I drive away. But the front landing is empty.

FIVE

Caitlin

I don't know what made my mood dip so quickly after Campbell parked the Range Rover in front of the house but I'm glad that he was quick to lift my spirits up the way he always does. But I also know part of the reason why. I hated that our time together was over so soon. I wanted to be with him all the way through evening and until the next day. It used to be so easy to hang out with him but that was before I saw him with just his towel on, before I smelled his scent on the bathrobe and his pillows. Or maybe it's just being alone again during the holiday that's finally getting to me.

I spot my parents' car from my bedroom window drive up the driveway fifteen minutes later. I'd just brought up the bags that Campbell had brought in and slipped on a pair of sweats. I meet them at the door, helping them bring in the presents and setting them on the space where my own bags from the holiday market had been.

"Where've you guys been?"

"We spent the night at your Aunt Millie's. No one wanted to quit playing pinochle," Dad says as he helps Mom with her coat.

"And then there was the rain," Mom adds.

"Didn't you get our message? We didn't want you getting worried spending last night alone in the house." Dad hangs Mom's coat behind the door and shrugs off his own.

I can't believe I never once glanced at my phone the whole time I was with Campbell. "I guess I missed it. Did you guys have fun?"

"Your mom won twenty bucks."

I glance at the old-fashioned answering machine on the console table, its light flashing to indicate they've got one message. Wanna bet it's from me letting them know I was spending the night at Campbell's.

"You lost twenty bucks so we're back to zero," Mom tells him, chuckling as they both head to the kitchen. "I'm going to warm some meatloaf, Cait. Your dad's starving. Have you eaten?"

"No, not since breakfast." I let my finger linger on the answering machine's Play button before pressing it, pressing Stop the moment I hear my voice. No, they don't need to hear that, definitely not when I don't even know what to think, my heart still racing at the mere thought of Campbell and the moment he winked at me when he caught me snooping on him in the bathroom. Something changed between us today and until I figure it out, I'm not saying anything to anyone. For all I know, it could just be my imagination. Maybe even wishful thinking.

"Then I'll make enough for all of us," Mom says as I join her in the kitchen. Dad walks to the living room and turns on the radio. Seconds later, holiday music streams from the speakers as he claims his spot in his favorite armchair and elevates his feet.

"Weren't you hanging out with Addy and Piper this week?" he asks from his spot.

"That's not till three days from now," I reply. "I actually can't wait to see Piper and be an aunt. She's like a mini-me."

Dad chuckles. "She sure is. Feisty like you, too."

"So how was your date with this Malcolm guy?" Mom asks, pots and pans clanging in her wake. "Did Roxy get it right this time?"

"Not really, but I had fun."

"As long as you had fun, then it's not really a disaster, is it?" Dad asks and I shake my head.

"No, definitely not a disaster."

As Mom turns on the oven and starts telling me about our cousins in New Jersey, I don't know why I'm keeping Campbell's name out of the discussion. I don't understand why I'm lying. Am I scared? Am I afraid they'd get angry if they found out? I know Jordan certainly won't approve. Or at least, he won't be happy knowing I'm putting his friendship with Jordan in jeopardy. What if Campbell and I don't work out?

But then, what if we do?

Two days later, Campbell picks me up exactly at six and he looks absolutely amazing in a midnight blue dress shirt that highlights his eyes and dark pants that emphasizes his muscled thighs and long legs. The sight of him standing at the door is even better than I imagined the past two days.

Hell, I've been barely able to sit still at all or focus, for that matter. Even Roxy became suspicious about how absent-minded I've been since she knew Malcolm and I didn't hit it off that night but she didn't push for details. But ever since the day I spent with Campbell, all I can think of is him, his rock hard abs, and those muscles. And his eyes... and his smile. I've even found myself going through the photos on my phone from years past, amazed at how I'd never really noticed just how hot he really is. It's not like I'm blind or that my man-radar is off, but maybe it's because he's Jordan's best friend and I know better than to imagine doing dirty things with him. Too bad I can't stop myself from doing just that right now.

"You look... stunning," Campbell says as we stand in front of each other, fidgeting. How long have I been standing at the door without saying a thing, too busy thinking about him and his blue eyes... and his abs?

"Thank you."

"Why the boots?"

I look down at my two-inch knee-high boots. "Anything wrong with them? They don't go with what I'm wearing?"

He shakes his head, chuckling. "They look great on you, Cait. Somehow, I thought you'd be wearing–"

"Stilettos, you mean, to go with the dress?" I say as he nods. "And tower over my date?"

"Not with me."

"Well, you're not the many guys I dated back in LA. Most of them were under 5'11. Not to say there's anything wrong with that... it just ruled out heels for me."

"Good for you, I'm not one of them," Campbell says. "You won't have to worry about that on our next no-date date."

"You remembered!" I love how cocky Campbell gets when he's not being Campbell, the boy next door.

"Why wouldn't I? You set the rules, remember?"

"I did, didn't I?"

He thrusts his hands in his trouser pockets and playfully takes a step forward. "Are there any rules to this no-date date I need to know about? I wouldn't want to break any of them."

The way he looks at me makes my mouth turn dry. It's a look he's never given me before, one that tells me he likes what he sees... and not in that 'she's my best friend's-sister' kind of way either. It's something else, one that makes my stomach do somersaults and my heart beat a bit faster. And I want more.

"Not really. But why don't we play it by ear tonight?" I whisper. "It'll be an experiment."

"I like the sound of that." His voice is deeper this time, huskier, his gaze lowering down my body and I bite my lower lip playfully, teasing him by shimmying my shoulders. He chuckles, his cheeks coloring as if I just caught him doing something he's not supposed to be doing before he peers over my shoulder. "Where's everyone?"

"My parents are at a Christmas party." I take a step forward so I'm inches in front of him. "I even told them not to wait up for me."

"You did?" His mouth is mere inches from my own, our noses almost touching. It's as if I'm caught in a trance under his gaze, broken only by my giggle.

"We're being silly, Campbell," I say nervously. "Are you ready?"

He clears his throat and takes a step back. "Yeah. Yeah, I'm ready."

The drive to the city is relatively quiet, the silence broken only by a debate on whether to listen to holiday songs or the current hits. We settle for whatever station he's already got saved and it happens to be a talk show.

"I like to keep up with the news," Campbell says when I glance at him. "So what have you been up to since I last saw you?"

"Just hanging out with Roxy and the girls," I reply, checking my nails. "We did more shopping and she taught me how to apply makeup like they do on those Instagram posts." I also got myself a Brazilian wax but that would have been too much information to spring on the guy on a date that's not supposed to be a date.

"The ones where their makeup's literally painted on?"

"Yup."

Campbell's eyes narrow. "Is that what you really want?"

"Not really."

"Then you don't need to do that, not unless you want to. I don't remember ever seeing you with a lot of makeup on, though. Either that or you do an amazing job making it seem like you're not wearing any."

I frown. "I don't know whether that's a good thing or a bad thing."

"I think you're beautiful just the way you are, Cait. Inside and out."

I feel my cheeks turn red. "No, you don't. You used to hate my guts when we were kids."

"That's when we were kids." He shifts his gaze back on the road before I can say anything, exiting 495W to Downtown and then to his apartment building where he parks his car. After helping me into my wool coat, we walk two blocks to a classic bar tucked away in a dark corner of Grand Central Terminal.

The moment we step out of a poorly marked elevator, I do my best not to stare. If this is a no-date date, then color me impressed... very impressed. With its 25-foot hand painted ceilings, a mahogany balcony, and a century-old leaded glass window and original millwork from the 1920's, I almost feel inadequate stepping inside. I've gotten so used to the casual vibe of Los Angeles that I've forgotten what New York grandeur feels like. And as Campbell guides me to one of the hunter green seated booths, it's also a world I'd never imagined him to feel at home in.

"Do you come here often?" I ask as soon as we're seated and he laughs.

"Wait! That should be my line."

"But I thought this was a no-date date."

"True, but if it makes you feel better, I meet my boss here sometimes and we discuss business," he says. "Portfolios, projections, and other stuff that'll bore you to tears if I keep going."

I almost tell him that he can bore me all he wants but that would mean amping up my flirt meter a hundred percent, even if we're already flirting right now. The sexual tension between us is so thick I could slice it with a knife.

"So after what happened the other night, I think I'll play it safe tonight," I say. "I'll have whatever you're having."

He cocks an eyebrow. "Whatever I'm having?"

"Yeah."

"I'm about to have a good stiff drink."

"Then I'm having one, too. Just one this time," I declare, determined to keep up with him.

"Lobster rolls or grilled cheese bites sound good to you?" he adds. "They only serve appetizers here."

"Sounds great."

Forty minutes later, I'm tipsy, sated, and my cheeks are hurting from all the smiling and flirting as Campbell hails a cab to get us to the theater on time. Between my first sip of Aviation, the cocktail he picked out for me, to the moment when he tucked an errant lock of hair behind my ear, I think we've clearly stepped beyond the line that marked us as just friends to something else.

By the time we make it to the theater, the mere brush of his hand on my elbow or my hand leaves me feeling giddy, and somehow I can't help but assume it's no longer accidental. Even the theater disappears whenever Campbell turns to look at me, all my senses heightened and focused on what he's doing, the words he's saying. When he holds my hand as we make our way to the lobby during the intermission, I don't see anyone else.

How long has it been since I've been with a man? Somehow I draw a blank. All I remember are the first dates that barely made it to first base, much less the second, my mind constantly on my research projects, meetings with my advisor, and that unwavering goal of making it to graduation and then finding a job.

But for tonight, I'm willing to toss all that out the window. I'm having way too much fun being with a man I've always felt safe with. Only this time, something's different. Somewhere between then and now, Campbell Murphy grew up and I never saw it until now.

SIX

Campbell

Why on earth did I have to pick *Coriolanus* for our first non-date date? Caitlin can't stop crying and I'm glad my boss had center row seats so no one has to scoot past us to leave the theater and I can just hold her as she talks about the things she loved about the play (everything), the lines that gutted her (a lot of lines) and the fact that she had to see her favorite actor play a betrayed general who gets killed onstage complete with fake blood. Ten minutes later, she dabs her tears with my handkerchief and blows her nose.

"Do you want this back?" She holds up the handkerchief and I shake my head.

"You can keep it."

She sniffs as she studies the embroidered initials on the fabric. "It's monogrammed."

"It's from my mother. She still gives me monogrammed everything for my birthday."

"Oh wow, she still does it," she whispers and I nod. "I thought she stopped doing that."

"Well, she still does." Even when she barely had any money, my mother always tried to find something to make me feel important. She knew how devastated I'd been after Dad left, shattered when she had to sell the house and find a live-in job as a cook for a rich family in the city because she didn't know how to do anything else. So even when money was tight because whatever she made went to the joint credit cards Dad had taken out without her knowledge, she'd buy plain handkerchiefs and embroider them with my initials for my birthday. She's since remarried, and while the handkerchiefs are no longer the cheap ones she used to buy at the dollar store, she still sews my initials on them herself.

"Thank you, Cam. This was just amazing. Now I can't get the lyrics out of my head."

"You're welcome, although I don't think there's anything wrong with lyrics being stuck in your head. Just don't suddenly break out in song. Or if you do, give me a warning." I move my arm from her shoulder. "You ready to head home?"

Caitlin's brow furrows. "You're taking me home already?"

"Actually, I was thinking maybe we could go to my

apartment and hang out a bit. Come to think of it, you never got to see the tree all lit up."

Caitlin bites her lower lip as she smiles. It's a playful smile that makes the knot in my belly tighten. "That's right. I haven't."

Suddenly all I see are the signs that I've fought so hard to ignore plain as day. How much longer can I go flirting with her when the last thing I want is to jeopardize my friendship with her older brother? Jordan is my best friend, or as he loves to say, my brother from another mother.

He helped get me through the toughest times in my life, brought me into his family and he trusts me with his sister. If I truly value my friendship with Jordan and his family, I need to put an end to this madness now. I need to stop stringing Caitlin along and make her believe something's going to happen between us.

But is that what I really want?

"Let's go," I say, my voice barely a whisper as I get up, knowing the moment I take her hand that there's no way I can let her go now.

We make it to my apartment in twenty minutes and by the time we walk through the door, we've had it with the self-control. I know I have. It took all of my willpower not to kiss her in the cab or the theater or the bar. It took the last thread of self-control not to kiss her in the elevator. But as soon as the door shuts behind us, it feels like a dam breaking and one touch of her hand on my face, stroking my stubble in the semi-darkness is all it takes for me to let go—that and thanking my lucky stars I hadn't set the timer for the Christmas tree or all this tension that's built up between us all night would have gone to hell.

"Cait..."

That's all I can say before I lower my head and kiss her. While I'd done my best to act cool around Caitlin the entire evening, it left a part of me almost distant, closed off only because I didn't know how she'd react. I kept second-guessing every touch, every smile, every time she snuck a glance at my direction during the play. When I held her hand, squeezing it as an emotional scene played onstage, I suddenly felt alive, as if a real live connection had been established between us. No more guessing.

But there's nothing like a kiss to seal the deal as I lose myself in the taste of her lips and the exquisite feel of her tongue. It's heaven in a kiss I'd never experienced before and like a man in search of the sublime, I want more. My hands move along her sides, slipping inside her coat to feel her soft curves and the warmth of her skin from underneath her dress.

"Our coats... they're in the way," she mumbles as she lets go of my neck and shrugs off her purse and her coat, her hands tugging at my shirt from under my coat.

"Cait, are you sure about this?" I ask as she pushes my coat off my shoulders.

She looks up at me with her big green eyes and my breath catches in my throat. God, she's beautiful.

So what the hell am I doing? Why the hell am I stopping her when this is exactly what I want, too?

"Just for tonight."

"And then what?"

"Then we can go back to the way we were," she whispers. "Don't you want to?"

I groan. "You have no idea how much I want you, Cait."

"Then stop talking and kiss me," she whispers fiercely as I respond with a kiss, this time deep and unforgiving. Her lips part, my tongue slipping between her teeth to taste her and savor every part of her that I can. We manage to get our coats off and then our shoes before I lift her in my arms, feeling her legs wrap around my waist as she holds on to me, our mouths still locked together, quenching fires that had been simmering all night long... no, ever since we spent the day shopping at the holiday market and I haven't been able to stop thinking about her. Her scent is intoxicating, the feel of her body electrifying against my own, so soft and curvy and sexy.

We stumble onto my bed, giggling as we land on the soft covers. I can't get enough of her. My mouth travels along her cheek to the sensitive skin behind her ear, feeling her shiver against me as I continue my exploration down her neck. Her hands undo the buttons of my shirt, tugging it loose from my pants.

"Roll over," she whispers and circling her waist with one arm, I roll onto my back while bringing her on top of me. As she straddles me, the lights from the neighboring buildings and the city below illuminate her exquisite form, casting her ginger hair in an ethereal glow.

I hold my breath, watching her slip off her dress in a slow striptease that makes me want to pull her down to the bed so I can take over. But I don't. I like watching Caitlin take charge. I love watching her be herself with me, only this time, in a way that's only meant for me.

Clad in only her bra and panties, she resumes her mission of getting my shirt off and with a little help from me, succeeds with a grin before blazing a trail of warm kisses on my neck and chest, all the way down my stomach. I'm so hard, her sex pressing against my erection not helping in any way. She's determined to tease and undress me and by God, I'm letting her do it.

Until I can't.

"You're determined to tease me, aren't you?" I murmur as she starts to unbuckle my belt, biting her lower lip in concentration.

"Maybe," she whispers. "I never realized you worked out. You're ripped."

I trace her thigh with my fingers. "Thank you. But you never asked."

"You never took your shirt off whenever you stopped by the house."

"I didn't have a reason to. Besides, it's also been a year since I've seen you. I missed you last time, remember?"

My belt buckle forgotten, Caitlin slides up my body so we're face to face again, her hair cascading along the sides of my face. I can smell her shampoo, sage and lavender. "Of course, I remember. I missed you. My partner in crime was MIA."

"I was working, but I missed you, too."

"No, you didn't. You were traveling. Italy from what I heard."

"Saint Lucia. But doesn't mean I wasn't working." I gather her hair in my hand and push it to the side as we lapse into silence. I can feel her watching me, studying me. "What are you looking at?"

"You," she replies, stroking my stubble with the back of her hand. "You're all grown up."

"I'm not the only one, Cait."

She bites her lower lip again, her gaze lowering down to my mouth. I can't believe we're doing this but it's also way past the point of no return. I don't think I can stop myself even if I want to.

"I want you, Cam. Just for tonight. And then–"

"And then what?"

"And then we'll figure it out later."

"Then stop talking and kiss me already, woman."

Caitlin chuckles. "Ooh, keep talking like that, and I just might."

I give her a playful spank on her buttock and she gasps, her eyes widening in surprise before I pull her down to kiss me, our tongues sparring, teeth mashing. This time I wrap my arms around her, one hand on the back of her head and the other on her hip, keeping her in place as she grinds her hips against me. I groan. There's no chance in hell this train's stopping now.

Holding her, I shift positions again, flipping her back on the bed. "No more talking," I murmur as Caitlin arches her back, helping me undo her bra. Her breasts spill out of their cups and I toss her bra to the floor. She moans as I squeeze them, pulling her nipples before I take one in my mouth, sucking and licking. She closes her eyes and brings her head back against the pillows. I do the same to the other nipple, feeling her body writhe beneath me. I move my head lower, zigzagging my tongue down her belly, my hand sliding lower and settling between her legs.

"Fuck, Cait. You're so wet."

"I thought you said no more talking," she gasps as my fingers slide along her sensitive lips.

"That was the exception." I kiss the skin just below

her belly button and she raises her hips, helping me lower her panties down her hips until she's completely naked before me. Gently, I nudge her knees apart, kissing the insides of her thighs as she giggles, my stubble grazing her skin.

Her clit is already swollen when my mouth descends on it, stroking her with my tongue as she whimpers, her fingers in my hair. I love the way she says my name, the way her hips buck beneath me as I slide one finger inside her and then another.

I'm taking a huge risk but I've made my decision. We both have and this is it. I feel her orgasm approaching, her back arching as I hold her thighs in place, hooking my forearms underneath her legs and holding her down. She tastes divine and I know once won't be enough. This won't be something that happens only one time, not when she's like a drug I'm not going to be able to quit so easily. When Caitlin comes, her body shudders and she falls back on the covers, pulling one of my pillows to muffle her cries. Her legs quiver in my grasp as I give her clit one more lick, one more suck between my teeth and she groans in frustration.

I get up from the floor and taking my wallet from my pocket, I unbuckle my pants, stepping out of them and my boxer briefs. When I straighten up, Caitlin watches me with wide eyes, her chest heaving as she catches her breath. Her gaze leaves my face, sliding lower down my torso. A half smile graces her lips as I slip a condom out of my wallet.

"You really are all grown up, Campbell Murphy, and in more ways than I can count."

"I didn't realize you were counting, Cait O'Halloran." I crawl on the bed between her legs. "I'll have to make sure you'll forget all about counting before we're done tonight."

She chuckles. "Is that a challenge?"

"You bet it is." I kneel in front of her, tempted to rip the condom wrapper before asking that question one last time. She's my best friend's sister, the girl next door I grew up with. We've hung out together, laughed, and argued. We've commiserated like thieves and gotten into trouble together more times than I can count. But we've never done anything like this. "Are you sure about this, Cait?"

Caitlin takes the foil wrapper from my hand, licking her lips as my cock juts in front of her like a steel rod. Any more talk and I'll be in trouble.

"Let me," she whispers, kissing the head of my cock, her tongue licking the precum glistening at the tip. I hold my breath, savoring the sensation of her warm tongue and her lips and now her hand, wrapping around the length of my dick, her other hand cradling my balls. Shit, if she doesn't hurry, I'm going to come. Foreplay is fine but in our case, that might as well have started hours ago.

"Cait..."

Her tongue cradling the underside of my cock, Cait takes me in her mouth slowly. I grip her hair with both hands, still kneeling in front of her as she repositions herself on all fours in front of me. The sight of her ass is enough to do me under. I'm losing all composure, the quantitative analyst that I am now reduced to the ordinary man he is underneath all the armor of designer clothes and thousand dollar wristwatches. They're all for show to the world to see but not to the woman in front of me. No, Caitlin has seen me at my most vulnerable. She's seen all of me before any other woman ever did. She's seen the broken boy that I used to be before I made the decision never to leave my fate in someone else's hands.

I pull away and Caitlin looks up at me, her brow furrowed. "I'm not going to last if you keep teasing me like that," I say, my voice gruff, all my muscles tensing. God, how much I want her.

She takes the hint and tears open the foil wrapper. Slowly she rolls the condom over my dick, her tongue pressed against the side of her lip as she focuses. Can condom rolling be any less romantic? But I also wouldn't have it any other way. I love the way she concentrates on my cock, like it's the most beautiful thing she's ever seen.

"Come here," I gently push her back down on the bed, our bodies coming together again, no more words forthcoming. Mouths meeting, teeth scraping, and tongues sparring. Our hands linger, stroke, and squeeze. Our bodies mold against the other like two halves becoming whole. When I enter her, she gasps and so do I. It's an exquisite feeling, heaven bottled in the few seconds our eyes lock together as I move deeper inside her, making sure she's okay. Her gasps make the pit of my belly tighten, her little moans music to my ears.

The next thrust comes harder and Caitlin whimpers, her fingers digging into the back of my shoulders.

"Fuck, Cait, you feel so good." Fast and slow, shallow and deep, I vary my strokes, feeling her pussy tighten around my cock with every thrust, her body shuddering as her orgasm nears. I kiss her, our eyes meeting, connecting. I want to tell her how beautiful she is, how she feels so right in my arms but there are no more words. Just this, our bodies meeting, coiling, coming together. She's tight. She's warm. She's perfect.

And as Caitlin comes, my name breathed against my mouth, she's mine.

When my own release comes, I bury my face in the delicate curve of Caitlin's neck, sinking my teeth into her soft skin. Nothing else matters but her.

SEVEN

Caitlin

Campbell finds me in the living room two hours later, sitting on the lambskin rug on the floor in front of his Christmas tree that's all lit up. Fully decked out with the decorations we'd purchased at the holiday market, he added white string lights that make the golden ribbons and tinsel glisten like stars.

"What are you doing here?" He settles on the rug behind me and brings the blanket over our shoulders, his body so warm against my back.

"I remembered the tree. I missed it on the way in."

"Ah, yes. I forgot to set the timer for the lights."

I turn to look at him, his stubble grazing my shoulder as he leans forward. "I found the switch for it and turned it on. Hope you don't mind."

"No, of course not. Thank you."

"You did a great job with it, Cam. It's beautiful."

"Thanks to you," he says, chuckling. "My mother's probably still in shock after I sent her pictures of it. She figured hell must have frozen over."

I giggle. "No, Caitlin just stormed through your apartment and demanded you put a tree up."

Campbell scoots forward, his legs on either side of me and his arms circling my waist. "Thank you for demanding I put a tree up. It's the best decision I ever made."

"To put up a tree for Christmas?"

"To be with you."

Suddenly it's as if he just said something he's not supposed to say. The reality of what just happened between us hitting me like a cold shower. "Well, about that..."

I feel Campbell's body stiffen though his arms remain where they are. "I thought it was just for tonight."

I nod. "Yes, just for tonight. I mean, I don't want what just happened between us to stand between you and Jordan. Your friendship is very important to him. To the family, and to me."

"As it is to me, too, Cait. I wouldn't do anything to jeopardize my friendship with him or your family... and that includes you."

So what just happened between us?

I turn my attention back to the tree, not wanting to

ruin a beautiful moment between longtime friends because in the end, that's what we are—friends. Who cares if we're sitting on a faux sheepskin rug buck naked? Besides, it had been my decision to have sex—and boy, other than the guilt I'm feeling right now, it was the best decision ever. I've always known Campbell to be this quiet, intense and driven kid and I'd never once considered him as anything but a friend mainly because I grew up with him. He's the boy next door... and whenever we get together, my partner in crime.

Who knew that between the sheets, he's amazing? His hands, his mouth, his... I bite my lip. No, better not go there.

Still, I may not have the experience to make such a declaration that he's an amazing lover—after all, I've only been with two men before tonight—but I've also never felt so comfortable, so sexy and so gorgeous with any man before. The way he makes love is just beyond words. And even if I could find the words, I won't because most of it can't be described using the alphabet, at least, not in a coherent arrangement.

I turn my head to look at him. I never realized how thick and long his lashes are. "I wanted it to happen, Cam."

Campbell kisses my shoulder. "I did, too."

I swallow nervously, our faces too close for two people who call themselves just friends, our lips inches away. I close my eyes, not knowing what to expect yet hoping that he kisses me. And he does, his arms tightening around my waist, pulling me against him.

Our kiss lasts for a few minutes, a combination of soft and feathery kisses, and sweet ones. None of the passionate deep kisses he gave me earlier, the ones that made my toes curl. I feel his hand cup my breast, his thumb and finger pinching my nipple.

Suddenly I pull away. My heart is pounding fast, as if there are a hundred horses galloping right under my ribs. "This isn't going to work, is it?" I ask hoarsely. "I'll always want more."

His hand leaves my breast. "Same here."

"It sucks because last night was… it was amazing."

"It was." He strokes my cheek. "So what do you suggest we do, Cait?"

I don't answer. I turn away to look at the tree again, needing to change the subject. "You forgot the star. The one that goes on top."

"No, I didn't." He leans away from me, reaching for something on the coffee table. It's a star ornament I'd picked out at the holiday market. I'd picked it specifically for the top of his tree. "I wanted you to have the honor of putting it up there. Thanks to you, I have a tree."

I take the ornament from his hand and get up from the floor, not caring if I'm naked. I want him to see me before we have to say goodbye to this little adventure, before we return to the way things were between us.

It shouldn't be too difficult to walk away from this, right? After all, we've always been good friends, able to tell each other anything and everything we want. That's why I'm so comfortable around him.

I stop in front of the tree and look back at Campbell. "Why don't we both do it together? It's your first tree, Cam. You should do the honors, but because I bugged you about it, then I can help put it up, too, as your partner in crime, so to speak."

"Troublemaker," he chuckles as he shrugs off the blanket from his shoulders and gets up from the floor.

The sight of him makes me catch my breath, my mouth turning dry. Goodness, but he does work out, doesn't he? Even his quads are toned, and his calves. Or maybe he runs. He always did like running. I force my gaze away from his legs, knowing I'm bound to let my gaze drift higher and I don't need the distraction.

As he stands behind me, he rests his hand on mine, his fingers holding part of the ornament. The warmth of his body is a welcome sensation against my shoulders and my buttocks and I close my eyes. Why does this feel so intimate? So special? Why do I keep wanting more?

Campbell rests a hand on my opposite shoulder. "You ready?"

Get your mind out of the gutter, Cait. "Yup."

As soon as we position the ornament on top of the tree, we both take a step back. "Thank goodness, this doesn't have those prickly needles," Campbell says as we both chuckle. String lights he'd arranged at the top of the tree illuminate the star perfectly.

"Merry first Christmas tree, Cam," I whisper. "It's absolutely beautiful. Like, social media worthy beautiful. If you have an account, we should take a picture for posterity's sake."

"I would but I wouldn't be focusing on the tree," he murmurs. "And I wouldn't be posting it anywhere either. It would be just for me... and you."

I feel my cheeks blush as I look away. "Oh, Cam, look at the tree. Focus."

"I am focusing." I can hear the dip in his voice. I can feel the charge in the air between us, intensifying with each passing minute. When our eyes meet, it's all I can do not to swoon. Campbell has a way of looking at a woman like she's the most beautiful thing in the world. This is what I get for not going out as much as I should have. I need more experience in the dating department to withstand Campbell as a lover. As a friend and the boy next door, I could totally handle him, but like this, it's impossible. Is that why Jordan always said that even though Campbell is often mistaken as quiet and introspective around our family, on his own, he's actually popular, especially with the ladies?

He takes a step closer and I force myself to keep my gaze on his face. Any lower and I'll really be in trouble. "If you really want me to focus on the tree, I'll do just that... unless you want me to focus on something else. Or do something else."

I bite my lip. This whole thing was my idea and tree or no tree in front of us, there's no way I'm letting go of it just yet. It's all or nothing. "Actually, I do."

"What is it?"

I turn to face him, the tree forgotten, and kiss him gently on the lips. "I want this." My lips travel down his neck, pressing against the pulse beating there. "And this." I feel his cock hardening against my belly. "I want more before we go back to the way things were between us."

Campbell wraps his arms around my waist. "Is that your final decision?"

I nod. "But if you don't want to do it again, I totally understand."

He exhales, chuckling softly against my ear. "That's the problem, Cait. Once you get a taste of something you've always wanted, it's difficult to walk away." His fingers push back my hair, exposing my neck to his mouth, his stubble tickling my skin. "But I understand why."

"So you're okay with it all?"

He nods, his finger lazily tracing my spine, goosebumps rising in its wake. His silence—words replaced by his hands doing the talking—is like a signal informing me that whatever I told him I wanted had officially begun. After all, I hadn't held anything back: I wanted him.

I hold my breath, closing my eyes as I allow my body to feel everything he's doing to me with just a touch of his finger. Why does my body feel so alive, so electric around him?

He pulls away, his fingers moving to my face, stroking my cheekbone before moving lower to trace the line of my collarbone. It's as if he's exploring me, memorizing me, and taking his time. His other hand takes mine and brings it to his lips, stubble grazing, scratching the back of my hand as his lips touch my skin. Then he rests my hand on his chest, as if letting me know he's not going to be the only one playing this game. It takes two.

I let my hand explore him, feeling the way his stomach tightens, my fingers tracing each indentation of his six-pack abs. My hand moves lower, gliding past his belly button, my wrist brushing against his erection.

"Cait..." he groans the moment I wrap my hands around his length, hot and hard against my palm, his skin like velvet. I open my eyes and see him watching me, his nostrils flaring. He says my name again and in his voice, I feel his need, his desire for me. It's unmistakable. How did I never see it before?

"Campbell..." I close the distance between us and let our actions speak instead, mouths meeting, bodies melting one more time before the morning comes and we'll have to go back to way things used to be.

I WAKE up the moment I see a sliver of sunlight streaking between the edge of the vertical blinds. We're back in his bed, worn out and smelling heavily of sex. Beside me, Campbell is asleep on his side, one arm tucked under his pillow and the other draped over my torso. His breath feels warm against my shoulder. I close my eyes as the memory comes, of us on the lambskin rug making love. Goosebumps dot my skin. Already I miss the feel of his lips on mine, his hands gripping my hair and his cock filling me completely. The thought alone makes me blush like mad as I slowly slip out of his arms and into the bathroom. Quietly, I get dressed, ignoring the butterflies in my belly fluttering like crazy as if protesting my planned departure.

I hate sneaking out like a thief but I promised Roxy I'd meet her for breakfast and the last thing I want her to see is me looking like I do with my mussed hair and raccoon eyes from my mascara. One look at me and I'm sure anyone would know that I just had a hell of an amazing night. But as I make my way down to the lobby and walk past the doorman, it hits me. How many women have walked out of Campbell's apartment like I just did?

I shake my head. *Stop it, Cait. Why should it matter if it's only going to happen for one night?*

The doorman hails a cab for me and I don't care about the cost to get back to Forest Hills. It beats riding the subway looking like I do, extending my walk of shame to the next borough in the bitter cold of winter. Already, it looks like it's getting ready to snow. It'll be the first time since I've been back in New York.

At least, it's early enough that traffic isn't as bad as it would have been if I'd waited. When I get home, the house is quiet and I hurry up to my room like a thief returning to his hideout with a secret stash. Only mine are made of contraband memories of one night that should never have happened.

EIGHT

Campbell

A TEXT MESSAGE WAKES ME UP AT ELEVEN IN THE morning.

Got time to hang out?

I reach my arm toward the space next to me and find it empty. Caitlin's gone, a strand of her hair on my pillow and the scent of sex still hanging in the air the only evidence she'd spent the night. I hate that I'm relieved that she snuck out of the apartment, as if her presence would have gotten me in trouble with Jordan this very minute even when he's nowhere near. But I also hate that she felt she had to leave without saying goodbye. We didn't even get to talk about what happened and what we should do next.

I scroll through the rest of my messages out of habit,

unconsciously ranking each of the three other messages according to their importance. The first is from last night, a holiday emoji from a woman I'd met at a bar while I was out with the office guys four weeks ago; the second is from Mitch at the office telling me there's some talk about a new office opening in Paris, and the third is from my mother, a brief video clip of a crocodile—or is it an alligator—walking on the golf course where she plays with her saying in voice-over, "Can you believe this, Cam? Only in Florida, right? Love you!"

I can't help but smile at her newly acquired knowledge on how to operate her smartphone but I admire her determination to get it right. At least, this time, her finger isn't covering the viewfinder.

I scroll back up to Jordan's text message and start typing my response.

Campbell: Yup, got the time. What's up?

Jordan: I need to get Addy a present. Thought I'd check out the holiday markets. You up for that?

Campbell: Sure. What time?

Jordan: In an hour. I'll meet you at your place.

I sit up. Shit, that would mean I'd have to explain

the damn tree. I've never had a tree in my apartment before and explaining how I got it would bring up Caitlin's name. There are also the obvious signs I've had a woman in the apartment—not that it's anything new since Jordan and I have hit the bars during the brief time he was single, after he finally called it quits with his childhood sweetheart Rachel and before he met Addison. But the woman in question is his sister. *Shitshitshit.*

Wait! Why the fuck am I acting so guilty?

Campbell: I'll meet you at the lobby. My place is a mess.

Jordan: You mean one cup didn't make it into the dishwasher before you ran a load and you're having an OCD moment?

I chuckle. My brother from another mother knows me too well. But I'm not really that uptight.

Campbell: Shut up. Lobby in an hour.

I toss my phone back on the bedside table and roll onto the other side of the bed, Caitlin's scent still lingering on the pillow. It brings back the memories of the last few hours, of us making love in front of the Christmas tree and then later on the bed. No holds barred fucking that left me breathless yet begging for more. She was insatiable, but then, so was I, and by the time we were done, it was almost morning and I could barely move. But now she's gone, our brief rendezvous over too soon.

I groan as the truth finally hits me like Mack truck, the empty side of her bed amplified a hundred times over. It was a one-time deal and now it's back to reality.

What the fuck did I just get myself into?

JORDAN MEETS me downstairs and we head out for lunch first, snow falling on the ground and dotting our wool beanies and coats with snowflakes. Knowing him, he's probably been awake since six or seven in the morning, bright and early like the contractor that he is, but at least, he understands my need for sustenance. I wake up early for work, too, but right now, I'm on vacation mode.

"Last minute shopping? That's not like you, man. You're usually prepared." I sit across from him at the corner diner, our booth situated right by the window where we have a view of the street.

"Try having a one-year-old living with you, Cam, and then talk to me about tackling your To-Do list. Time isn't your own anymore and there's also the wedding," he says, laughing. "If Addy and I could elope and just get it over with, we would."

"But her mother will kill you."

"She sure will. And Mom and Dad are kinda into it now. Actually, they kinda like it." He pauses, chuckling. "They figure it'll prepare them when it's Cait's turn. Wanna bet? With her, they'll probably go all out."

Hearing her name sends my heart racing but I do my best to act nonchalant. Our arrangement was for one night, not a lifetime. I clear my throat, my mouth suddenly feeling dry. "That would be interesting, wouldn't it? Seeing Caitlin getting married."

"Only if she finds a man who can handle her. She can be a spitfire, my sister, in case you haven't noticed," Jordan says. "She knows what she wants and she doesn't let anything stop her from getting it. But you already know that."

"I'm sure she'll find her perfect match."

"True, and he's got to be someone who can tell her what to do for a change. Knowing her, she'd probably end up not wanting a wedding because she'd worry about the cost," Jordan says. "But it would be nice to see Dad walk her down the aisle. He's actually looking forward to it... and more grandkids."

I force a smile, imagining Caitlin in a white dress even though I can't get myself to see who'd be waiting for her at the altar—nope, can't do that because what we had was an experiment, a one-time arrangement. Then I remind myself not to think of her at all. Or about weddings and babies.

"I'm not sure she'd like all the attention though," Jordan continues, his brow furrowing. "You know how she is about money. She'll think the costs associated with a wedding would be better put toward a house or living expenses for a year. She's been pretty frugal lately." He pauses when the server arrives to take our order before resuming once she walks away. "I told her she should take a vacation after she graduates, like I did when I took that year off. She deserves it."

"You didn't exactly take a vacation, man. You were building schools in third world countries... with no power tools," I say. "That's not exactly a vacation."

He laughs. "To you, it isn't. Let's call it a working vacation. I had a blast."

I chuckle. Classic Jordan, always busy with his hands, always wanting to help others. "What did Caitlin say about the vacation thing?"

"She wants to work and kinda start paying her way," Jordan replies. "I just feel bad I took a year off and she kept chugging along with her studies. And she still is. But Mom and Dad have set aside enough money for her and a friend to go on a vacation for a couple of weeks. Nothing crazy, but a vacation nonetheless. Addy and I pitched in, too."

If I had my way, I'd pay for her whole vacation. A

few weeks taking her to her favorite place is a fraction of my bonus. But knowing Caitlin, she'd only feel insulted if I offered especially after what happened between us. But maybe not if I take her with me on that vacation, something that goes beyond a one-night arrangement, something I absolutely wouldn't mind at all. "She's graduating a month after your wedding, man."

"Yeah, we'll be in LA then for her big day," Jordan says. "You planning to attend her graduation, right? I'm sure she'd like to see you there, too."

I nod. I'd already put it on my calendar. "I wouldn't miss it for the world."

The server arrives with cups of steaming hot coffee and sets them on the table in front of us. "What have you been up to on your vacation, man? Seeing anyone new?"

"Catching up on sleep. That's it, pretty much. Oh, and hanging out with you." It's a lie but that's all I can think of before tackling my coffee. And for the next half an hour, we focus on eating, talking about what he's up to now that he's got a fiancée and a baby to keep him busy, and what time the Christmas Eve dinner at his parents' house will begin. They used to have dinner on Christmas Day but with Addison's parents holding their own dinner on Christmas Day, the O'Hallorans compromised. This year, they'd hold dinner on Christmas Eve instead and the next day, they'd attend the Rowe's.

"It will be crazy like always, but that's family for you, man. And that includes you, brother from another mother," Jordan says, grinning. "How's your mom?"

"She's great. Golfing like crazy, as always." I pull out my phone and play the clip she sent me that morning. Jordan takes the phone and plays it again, amazed, before handing the phone back to me.

"Heard from your dad?"

I hate that he asks the question no one dares to ask but I also appreciate that he does. Sure, a part of me hates Dad's guts for leaving us the way he did but there's also that part of me that wants to know why. Did I do something wrong? Did Mom? Was I just not good enough?

"Did hell freeze over?"

Jordan shrugs. "Guess the answer's no."

After lunch, we head to the Columbus Circle Holiday Market where Jordan wasn't joking about needing to do his last-minute holiday shopping. He goes at it with such determination that it looks like he's got everything mapped out—which stalls to visit first complete with a break for hot chocolate and churros along the way. Two hours later, he seems to have found everything: organic baby clothes and a stuffed bunny toy for Piper, a fair trade silk and cotton shawl for Addison, a ceramic bowl for his mom, a handmade leather portfolio for his dad, and a pair of felted owl slippers for Caitlin.

"What about me, man? How come I don't get anything? You just hurt my feelings." I say, feigning sadness as we make our way down the subway. Jordan's next stop is the supermarket close to their Chelsea apartment where he wants to get ingredients to make a roast.

"Yeah, right," Jordan says. "How do you know I didn't snag you something when you weren't looking? Hand-knit wool socks with tiny llamas from Peru, maybe?"

"Ah, never mind."

"Seriously, I hear girls like them on guys."

"Shut up."

It's the usual ribbing we do together, like the brothers we've become ever since Jordan asked his parents if I could live with them since they had a guest room that was only being used as storage for toys he and Caitlin had outgrown. The room had everything a teenage boy would need, a bed, a dresser, even a desk facing the backyard and a bookshelf. My mother, broke and with limited options, accepted their offer. After all, she was working in the Hamptons and that left me either following her there and transferring schools or finding a room for me to rent in Queens.

Through it all, not once did Jordan or Caitlin tell anyone at school about my circumstances. To them, me moving in seemed like the most natural thing in the world and there's no denying how much their family shaped who I am today. That means no matter what happened last night between Caitlin and me, there's no way I'm going to jeopardize that.

NINE

Caitlin

The moment I get home, I take a shower and dive into the warmth of my bed even for just an hour or two. My body is sore and tender, the hours of love-making taking its toll and all I want to do now is sleep all day. I still need to meet Roxy for breakfast and then Addison at noon and so I need to catch up with my beauty sleep before anyone can tell that something's amiss.

It's also a relief to know that Jordan's not going to be hanging out with us. After last night, I don't want to lie about my feelings for his best friend.

After breakfast with Roxy where she tells me all about the latest cocktail she's mastered, I remind her to show up at the house on Christmas Day so she can pick up her presents. She's always running about that I never know what's going on with her so it's usually better when she drops by when she can rather than having me catch up with her at her apartment. Then I hurry to the subway and make my way back to Manhattan, this time to Chelsea.

Addison—with Piper snug in the carrier—is raring to leave the apartment and hang out the moment I arrive. I love that my future-sister-in-law is smart and funny, the perfect match for Jordan who can be just as hilarious when he wants to be.

Addison is a Filipino-American nephrologist with a private practice she runs with two other doctors. Her and Jordan's paths would never have crossed but somehow they did. One day, she and my brother met at a small bar close to his apartment and from that moment on, he was smitten. She even got him to sing a karaoke duet with her, *I Got You Babe* by Sonny and Cher. That alone is a feat because Jordan never sings, not for anything or anyone.

From what I've been told, they had a one-night stand two days before Jordan left for Asia to work with a non-profit. When he got back, he found out he had a daughter, Piper, who looks just like he and I did when we were babies. A redhead with intense green-hazel eyes. There was never any doubt Piper was his and Jordan took responsibility right away. I've never seen him so in love with a woman since Rachel, his childhood sweetheart of almost five years and the daughter of

Dad's business partner. They'd broken up three months before he met Addison and just like that, all it took was a chance meeting at a karaoke bar.

Isn't that what's going between Campbell and me? A chance meeting at his company holiday party that led me to spend the night at his apartment and see him in a different light the morning after? Is that all it takes? Chance?

Or in our case, a lot of sneaking around?

The three of us spend the afternoon at the Whitney Museum of Art and a short walk on the High Line to enjoy the sight of birds enjoying winterberries before heading back to their apartment for dinner. It's a laid-back afternoon that has me forgetting everything else but art and the joy of being around babies. I love playing aunt to Piper who's already got the fine art of charming everyone around her down to a science.

"You okay?" Addison asks when we're two blocks from the apartment. "You've been quieter than usual. Something bothering you?"

"Not really. Just..." I pause, not knowing what to tell her. "Can I ask you a question?"

"Sure."

"How did you know my brother was the one?"

Color creeps on Addison's cheeks as she gazes at Piper who's asleep in the baby carrier in front of her. "I actually didn't think he was the one when I first met him. I did think he was the hottest guy I'd ever met, though. Not a lot of doctors are built like your brother," she replies.

"I'm actually glad you guys are together," I say. "It's like you're both meant for each other."

Addison blushes even more. "Anyway, I'd gone into that bar to blow off steam and we met and we hooked up. That was supposed to be it. I'd never had a one-night stand before, come to think of it, and that's why when he asked for my number, I tried to play it cool and not give it to him. When I realized I was pregnant and he was MIA, I had it in my head to go ahead with the pregnancy and raise Piper all by myself with the help of my family."

"It must have been hard."

She nods. "A little bit. But it wasn't until he walked into my office a year later that I realized he wasn't just gorgeous, he was kind. He was responsible. I think that does something to women, the knowledge that here's a man who'll move heaven and earth to make sure you're provided for and safe, like the way pheromones can cause an emotional almost primal reaction between humans."

"I know he's crazy about you."

"Anyone who's brave enough to go through the wedding arrangements with my mother and all the drama associated with it has got to be. And I'm glad he's game. He's actually the only man I've known who can handle my mother. He's also my soulmate. It's a feeling you can't explain, where you know things are going to be alright when you see each other," Addison says, her gentle smile conveying so much more. Heck, the fact that my brother, who never cooks, actually made dinner speaks volumes. "Anyway, why do you ask?"

I shrug. "Just curious."

We don't speak for a while, too busy navigating the holiday crowds in front of a holiday market. But as soon as we clear the block, she continues, "What about you? Are you seeing someone?"

"Kinda but it's just casual."

"How casual is casual?" she asks as she adjusts Piper's wool hat.

"He's a friend."

"Ah. Friends with benefits."

"You could say that. Only I don't want our benefits to jeopardize the friendships around us," I continue. "I mean, we're not the only ones who are friends. We have mutual friends, too."

"Are you afraid your arrangement will complicate things with everyone else?"

"Don't they always?"

Addison thinks for a few moment. "Not unless they keep it quiet or maybe they'll come out and say they're madly in love with each other and can everyone just please be happy for them."

"We're not at that point yet. Not even close."

"Would you want to get to that point?"

Her question catches me by surprise but I don't answer. We've arrived in front of her apartment building situated on a tree-lined block now covered with snow, saying hello to the doorman who opens the door for us. I'd originally planned on saying goodbye outside but there's also her last question.

"I'm not sure yet if I want to be or not," I reply when we're inside the elevator. "I don't want to mess up the status quo if we don't work out in the end."

"Ah, that." Addison chuckles, gently covering Piper's ears, her voice lowering as she continues. "Sometimes you gotta fuck status quo and just do it, you know? You never know it just might work."

As she opens the door to the apartment, we find ourselves face to face with Campbell who is buttoning his wool coat, a beanie covering his head. Jordan is in the kitchen and the apartment smells of pot roast.

As Addison says hello and breezes past Campbell, I stop at the landing and do my best not to stare. He looks just as surprised as I am.

"Hi," he mumbles as behind him, Jordan helps Addison remove a still-sleeping Piper from her carrier.

"Hi."

"Please don't tell me you're leaving, Cam." Addison says as she slips the empty baby carrier off her shoulders. "Aren't you staying for dinner?"

"He's been dying to leave for the past half hour but I needed him to help me with dinner since he paid more attention to Mom's cooking tips than I ever did," Jordan says before disappearing into the nursery with Piper.

"Jordan wanted to surprise you by making dinner," Campbell says. "I just figured I'd give you guys some privacy."

"Privacy Shmivacy. Tell Piper that," Addison says, laughing. "Anyway, stay and join us, Cam, unless you've got a date or something." She pauses, turning to face me. "I hope you'll stay, too, Cait. I'd love to talk more about your dissertation."

As I open my mouth to say no, that I'm busy—doing what, I have no idea, maybe I'll finally learn how to crochet something—I know it's rude and cowardly. I'm also not the type to run away from things like this.

"Sure, I'd love to," I hear myself say as Campbell, his gaze never leaving me, shrugs off his coat and hangs it behind the door.

"Just like old times," he says as I glare at him, the temptation to pull him to me and kiss him growing greater with each passing second.

When Jordan returns to the kitchen, Campbell and I help him set the table and I'm grateful for a task... any task to keep my mind off what happened last night even though it's useless, for here Campbell is in the flesh, tempting me with his charming smile, those hard six-pack abs hiding beneath his light blue shirt and a firm ass that has the audacity to be covered by jeans.

While dinner is "just like old times," it also isn't. For how can it be like old times when all I can think of whenever I look at Campbell sitting next to me is the way he kissed me last night. And when his hand brushes against mine as he passes the salt or the salad is how he made me feel so beautiful when he held me, his lips against my ear whispering words I'd never heard him say before when we were just friends. I'm simply too distracted, betrayed by my body and my mind that used to have no problems discussing gene mutations that increase the risk of cancer just before I got on the plane to New York. Instead, all I can think of now is the sound of Campbell's voice when he groaned my name.

By the time we both walk out of Jordan and Addison's apartment two hours later, my smile is just a little too broad and my voice a little too loud to mask all the giddiness I'm feeling inside.

"Hey, Cam, you're gonna drop her off, right?"

Jordan calls out from his front door as Campbell and I head toward the elevator.

"I can make my way home on my own no problem, Jory. No need for a chaperone." I punch the elevator button. It's not as if Jordan hasn't asked the same favor from Campbell so many times in the past; it's just that things are different now and I can't help but feel defensive. I can find my own way home, thank you very much.

"Yeah, I'll drop her off, man, no problem."

"Thanks." Jordan gives him a thumbs up before closing the door and for the next few seconds, Campbell and I glare at each other until the elevator doors slide open.

But all that suppressed tension fades away the moment the doors slide close. Suddenly, all my self-control is gone… just gone. And so is Campbell's. I lean against the back wall of the elevator as he steps toward me, his blue eyes seeing right through me. I feel his fingers stroking my cheek first and when I close my eyes, the warmth of his lips on mine. The feel of his stubble comes after, when my lips part and his tongue slips between my teeth, probing, searching, claiming. His other hand slides along my waist, pulling me to him, possessive. I smell his cologne, the scene awakening all the sensations from last night when he took me to the edge and then back again and again until I begged him to let me come. Why does it feel as if the man I'd been searching for in others back in LA was right in front of me all along?

As my arms circle his neck, Campbell pulls away, out of breath, studying me. "I should take you home. I promised Jordan I would."

"He didn't state a time, did he?"

"No."

"That means you can drop me off in the morning. It'll still count."

His eyes narrow as he gazes at me. "But I thought we agreed it was just for one night. Our little experiment to get it out of our system."

The elevator doors slide open and thankfully, no one is waiting to get in. "I think I'm going to need one more night to get it completely out of my system. What about you?"

"You know the answer to that, Cait," he murmurs, his gaze fixed on me as the butterflies in my belly go crazy and I giggle.

"Then what are we waiting for?"

We get to his apartment in record time—fifteen minutes. We undress each other for a lot less, scarves, coats, long johns (because we've both been out and about), boots, and everything else—seven minutes. We're expedient until we don't need to be, the feel of his skin like a balm to the emptiness I've felt since I left his apartment this morning, and this time, it's him leaning against the wall as I kiss and lick my way down his torso. I want to hear him beg. I want to listen to him groan my name, feel his fingers in my hair, guiding me where he wants me to be.

His cock is glorious and perfect, throbbing as I gently press my lips against it. He hisses when I move lower to lick his balls.

He groans, bringing his head back as I wrap my hand around the base of his cock and lick his length starting from the base, my tongue swishing side to side as I take my time.

Campbell groans again, grabbing my hair and then letting go. I see his abs tense, feel his thigh muscles tighten. I love the sounds he makes, the way his body trembles beneath my touch.

When I get to the tip and swirl my tongue around the head of his cock, he gasps, watching me with lidded eyes, his nostrils flaring. "Fuck, Cait. We're in so much trouble."

I withdraw, licking the underside of his cock. "We'll worry about that tomorrow."

"Yeah," he gasps again as I take him in my mouth, loving the sounds he makes as I suck and lick him. I want to do everything we're not supposed to be doing, experience pleasures I've only dreamed of doing with him before reality sets in again in the morning and family will have to come first. We can do it, I know we can.

We just have to get through tonight first.

THE NEXT MORNING, Campbell and I hardly look at each other or even talk. Sure, we do the usual *good mornings, how are you* bit but that's about it. It's as if the clock has struck twelve and he's on a mission to take Cinderella home seven hours too late.

He plays R&B on the radio and I busy myself by watching the city cloaked in snow pass outside the window. I wish I could rest my hand on his forearm like I used to when I had something to say or crack a dirty joke and think nothing more of it. It would have been completely normal, just two old friends hanging out.

But Campbell was right that first night. Once you get a taste of the forbidden, there's no way you can go back to not wanting it again... and again.

At least, we got some sleep this time. And as if to make sure I wouldn't sneak out of his apartment like I did the day before, Campbell held me all night and never let go until morning.

Still, I can't deny the sense of loss I'm feeling, as if I'm making the biggest mistake in my life. Why is it that the man who suddenly sets my heart racing is the same man I grew up with? What did I miss? What didn't I see all those years? Or wasn't I just paying attention?

By the time he turns toward Forest Hills, panic hits me. I glance at the clock on the dashboard.

Nine o'clock.

It means Mom and Dad are awake and they're sure to see me come in.

"Shit," I mutter under my breath.

"What is it?"

"Mom and Dad are probably downstairs getting everything ready for tonight."

"And?"

"Can you drop me at the Jefferson's?"

Campbell frowns. "That's five houses away, Cait. Are you sure? I can drop you off at the house. No big deal. I promised Jordan I'd drop you off and that's exactly what I'm doing."

"I know, but I don't want them seeing you drop me off this early."

"Then we should have considered that last night before we–"

"Before we what?" I exclaim angrily. "Before we fucked each other's brains out? It's too late for that, Campbell."

His jaw clenches but he doesn't say anything.

"Look, Cam, just drop me off at the Jefferson's. Please."

"Cait, you're not some cheap date I just drop off around the corner and leave. You're my—"

"—best friend's sister," I say angrily. "That's what I am, Cam, and yes, you're going to have to drop me off at the Jeffersons because I don't want to jeopardize your friendship with my brother and my family. I thought we discussed this already. We agreed on a fling and this is pretty much it. End of the line."

Campbell takes a deep breath and for a second, I almost think he's going to drive directly to my house but he doesn't. He slows down the SUV and stops right in front of the Jeffersons. When I push open the door, he touches my forearm. "Cait, listen to me. I want to tell Jordan about us—"

"No!" I glare at him. "Cam, what we had was just temporary. That's it. Besides, I'm going back to LA after the New Year and work my ass off until I graduate so I can start working and actually be of use to my family for a change instead of just going to school all the time. The last thing I need is a distraction."

"Is that what I am to you? A distraction?"

"I never said that."

"You just did, Cait."

I push the door open and step out, grabbing my wool coat from the back seat and slipping it on while ignoring him. Guilt fills me... and fear. I look at him, my hand on the door. "Please don't let this change anything between us, Cam."

"Everything changed the moment we decided to take this step, Cait. Don't you get it? This isn't just one of those wham-bam-thank-you-ma'am deals. Not anymore."

"Well, it may not be to you but I'm not ready to lose all the years you, me, and our families have built," I say.

"Who says we're going to lose it? I'd rather be honest than—"

"And I'd rather not, Cam. Not right now." I pause, hating that I can't think straight... or see clearly for that matter. *Am I honestly about to cry?* "Look, Cam, please don't let this change anything between us." When he doesn't answer, I continue, "I hope to see you tonight. Everyone will be expecting you like always."

Campbell turns away from me, muttering something that sounds like "yeah" before I close the door and start walking away. I don't hear him drive away but I don't turn around to look either. I just keep walking, hating myself for the things I just said as if what we had wasn't special at all, but I'm also relieved that he didn't argue with me. It's for the best anyway. We both need things to go back to the way they were.

I know I do.

TEN

Campbell

I almost back out of Christmas Eve dinner at the O'Halloran's but I don't. I can't. They're not just my family, they're my lifeline all year round. I don't just show up for Christmas Day, I'm there for Thanksgiving, birthdays, even baptisms. And on the day before Christmas, I'm there early helping Mrs. O'Halloran with dinner just as I'd promised her the year before. That's when I said out loud that I wanted to learn how to recreate a full Christmas dinner and the challenge was on. She hasn't forgotten and neither have I.

Sometimes, when Mrs. O'Halloran has a new recipe she wants to share with me, she'll have me come over to pick up portions set aside in plastic containers to take home. I'm not Jordan's brother from another mother for no reason at all. They took me in when I had nowhere to go. They treated me—and still treat me—like their second son.

There's no way I'm ruining everything over a fling. Like Caitlin said, everything needs to go back to the way it was.

I arrive at their house at ten, my dress shirt and trousers in a garment bag that I hang in the guest room for later, the presents I've picked out for the family arranged under the tree with all the others. In the kitchen, Mr. O'Halloran is already helping out, studding the ham with cloves.

I join them in the kitchen wearing a long-sleeved shirt and jeans. "Where's Caitlin?"

"She and Roxy went out to do last minute shopping," her mother replies. "The poor girl only got today off from the hospital and she has to go in again tomorrow afternoon. So Cait offered to help her battle the crowds."

Mr. O'Halloran chuckles. "It's going to be hectic out there but those two ladies can handle themselves."

"Do you think you can handle being in here, Campbell?" Mrs. O'Halloran asks, grinning. "It'll be hot in the kitchen, I guarantee you. I'll be putting you to work, young man."

Laughing, I slip on the apron Mr. O'Halloran hands me, grateful for the distraction of not seeing Caitlin everywhere I look. Of course, I'm up to the challenge, anything that will take my mind off their daughter. "Then bring it on, Mrs. O."

Five hours later, the party is in full swing and everyone is home, even Caitlin who arrived while I was taking a shower in the guest bathroom. Music is playing and the tree is all lit up, more presents set underneath the tree as the Rowes are last to arrive. On the floor, Piper is the center of attention with both sets of grandparents and she's loving it.

Jordan hands me a beer as soon as I make it downstairs wearing jeans and a dark knit shirt. "Merry Christmas, man. Here's to family."

We tap bottles. "Family. Merry Christmas."

He takes a sip before glancing toward the living room. "Gotta give you a heads up. I hear Addy's mom wants to pair you with one of her nieces, Emily, who's in town for a few months. Addy's horrified, of course, but I'm sure her mother will find a way to say something over dinner."

I chuckle. "I'll be ready."

"You're not seeing anyone, are you?"

I open my mouth to say no but stop myself. "Not exactly."

Jordan grins. "Anyone I know?"

Before I can lie to my best friend, his parents call us over to join them in the living room and I heave a sigh of relief. Crisis averted, the inevitable lie delayed.

But where the hell is Caitlin?

Half an hour later, Caitlin comes downstairs to join us at the table. She's wearing a red dress that fits her like a glove, its skirt flaring down her hips just past her knees. It takes all my willpower not to stare at her ass but I manage, forcing myself to pay attention on everything around the table but her—Mr. and Mrs. O'Halloran insisting on serving everyone even when Jordan tells them to sit down and take it easy, Mrs. Rowe doing the same thing until Addison orders her to sit down and eat. And then there's Piper smearing mashed potatoes in her hair.

But even with all the commotion, it isn't easy not to look at Caitlin, not when she's sitting right beside me like she always does year after year. Before this moment, we'd probably be cracking jokes at each other, teasing each other over what we did during the year. By now, I'd probably be pouring wine into her glass like it's nothing and put my arm around her like a friend. Because that's what she was until two nights ago. I still pour the wine and offer her the appetizer, but she refuses to look me in the eye, her gaze directed at my mouth or my nose and never my eyes, as if she's hiding something... as if she's guilty.

Hell, we both are.

But I can't help but want her to look at me. Just once. She's simply stunning, her green eyes sparkling and her red hair falling over her shoulders in waves. And then there's the Santa hat she's wearing that makes me want to reach over and play with the little pompom at the tip of it. She's barefoot, too, for shoes aren't really required when she's already home, and when she folds her legs underneath her and I catch sight of her cute painted toes, I can't look away.

Why do I suddenly want to announce to everyone that—

"Campbell, could you pass the beans, please?"

I turn to Addison sitting across from me. "Sorry. What?"

"The green beans." She points to the green bean casserole in front of me and I hand it to her. Beside her, Jordan is watching me.

Pay attention, man, before you really spill the beans and mess up everyone's Christmas.

"I hear you're about to graduate in a few months," Mr. Rowe says. "You're majoring in Molecular Biology, right? I think that was one of the majors Addison was considering before she settled for Biology."

"Yes. I graduate in the summer."

"Any work prospects? You going to stay there?" he asks.

"Whoever offers me the best opportunity," Caitlin replies, pausing to pass the bowl of mashed potatoes to Jordan. "My priority is to get a job—any job—so I can start paying my way."

"Not when you earned that scholarship, Cait," Mr. O'Halloran says. "So the last thing I'd worry about is working. One more semester."

"Yeah, one more semester," she says, chuckling. "I can't wait."

"Who knows? You could find Mr. Perfect over there and get married," Mrs. Rowe says. "Guess what, I know this young man at church who would be the perfect match–"

"Ma!" Addison groans. "No matchmaking tonight, okay?"

"You're pretty quiet, Campbell," Mr. O'Halloran says. "The boss doesn't have you working during Christmas Eve, I hope?"

"No work, Mr. O. I'm actually on vacation for the first time in years."

Mrs. O'Halloran looks surprised. "Really? That's a first. But I bet you're still working from home."

"I don't know if I'd call it work but it's the usual. Read, study the market, analyze companies and all that but it's not exactly work-work, like doing modeling and compiling reports," I reply.

"That's work!" Mrs. Rowe says, laughing. "I've got

someone in mind for you Campbell. My niece, Emily, who just moved–"

"Ma, no matchmaking, please," Addison says again.

"No, I'm really just kinda hanging out, Mrs. O," I say. "I even put up a tree."

The silence that follows me surprises me and as I look around the table, all I see is everyone's stunned expressions staring right back at me... except for Caitlin who's staring at the food on her plate.

I wipe my mouth, setting the napkin back on my lap. "Did... I say something wrong?"

Jordan: Dude, you got a tree? Are you serious? I thought you didn't like pine needles all over your apartment.

Addison: It depends on the type of tree. Some have needles falling everywhere and some don't.

Mr. O'Halloran: Wow. That's a first. You've never had a tree at your apartment before, have you?

Mrs. O'Halloran: I thought you told us once that your apartment was too small for a tree.

Addison: You can have a tree in a small apartment. A small tree.

Mrs. Rowe: True, but it's not the same as a big tree. The one you have here is huge. It looks like it's been stolen from a Bergdorf Goodman's window.

Mr. Rowe: Amelia...

Mrs. O'Halloran: Did you know about this, Cait?

That Campbell got a tree? Do you have anything to do with it because you two can be thick as thieves–

"Guys, it's just a tree," I say, shrugging. "Figured it's never too late to get into the holiday spirit. Besides, I'm on vacation and it's fun to do something different for a change."

"Is that why you didn't want me to come up yesterday? Because you got yourself a tree?" Jordan asks, his eyes narrowing. "Then it's got to be because of a girl then. Who is it, man? Anyone I know?"

"I think it's a great idea to do something different during the holidays," Addison says. "Kinda like surprising yourself."

"What about you, Caitlin? Mary told me you went out on a blind date a few days ago," Mrs. Rowe says. "How'd it go?"

"That didn't work out," Caitlin replies matter-of-factly.

"Why? Was he being a jerk to you?" The question comes from me and she looks at me in surprise.

"No... not exactly," Caitlin stammers.

"Not exactly?" Jordan doesn't sound amused. "Either he was or he wasn't being a jerk to you, Cait. Is this the same guy that Roxy paired you with? She might need to give up on the matchmaking. It's not her strong suit."

"No, he wasn't a jerk. Well, not exactly," Caitlin replies, her brother's second question unanswered.

"If he wasn't, why end it?" I ask, ignoring the dagger look I'm getting. "You didn't like him?"

"Because holiday romances don't last," she replies, not looking at me. "They just don't."

"Says who?" Addison asks.

"Says me," Caitlin replies. "I mean, Christmas romances are like vacation romances. There's this spike of dopamine and adrenaline from knowing someone for such a short amount of time but then the vacation is over and that's it. Reality sets in and you realize that other than that initial burst further enhanced by the Christmas spirit, it's not something that can last long-term."

"What's dopamine?" Mrs. Rowe asks. "Is it like doping?"

"No, Ma," Addison replies. "Doping is another word for drugs."

"So maybe with this guy, it is short term but that doesn't apply to every guy," Mrs. Rowe says. "I can find you someone at the church social."

"No, Amelia," Mr. Rowe says. "No matchmaking."

"That's a very strange way of looking at it, Cait," Mr. O'Halloran says before asking Jordan to pass him the cranberry sauce. "But did you like him, at least? Did you guys get along until this... this reality set in?"

"I did like him, but not enough to get all torn up about it ending so soon, you know?" Caitlin replies as I do my best not to glare at her, the words she just uttered like a knife twisting in my chest.

"Knowing when to move on is really important and I'm glad you recognized it wasn't working, Cait," Mrs. O'Halloran says. "You're beautiful, smart, and one day, you'll find Mr. Right, not Mr. Right Now."

Everyone around the table nods their head in agreement except for Piper who's happily smearing mashed peas all over her face until Addison puts a stop to it, and for the rest of the dinner, all attention is on the baby.

I move my food around my plate, my appetite gone even though I came to the party hungry.

"It's better this way, Cam. You know it is and this is what we agreed on." Caitlin's not looking at me as she speaks. She's watching everyone fuss over Piper.

"People change their minds, Cait."

"I'm heading back to LA in a week and you've got work so it's not like it was ever going to work between us anyway. There's also Jory and my family." She pauses, sighing. "I don't want to lose you and all this because of a fling, Cam. You're family."

"If I'm family, then why can't you even look at me as you say that?"

She turns to look at me, her green eyes flashing. "Is that better?"

I look away, the urge to get up from the table growing with each passing second. Caitlin and I have had our disagreements before but we hadn't slept together then. This one is different; it's personal and it stings.

And she's right. The O'Hallorans are the only family I have and I don't want to lose them either. Already, Caitlin and I aren't working out anyway. She couldn't even look me in the eye until a few seconds ago, as if all the years where we sat next to each other every Christmas laughing and joking are now a distant memory. I can't even touch her without remembering the two nights we spent together and the way her body responded to mine, how perfectly she fit against me like she always belonged in my arms from the beginning.

But if this is what she wants, then I'm fine with it. It's not as if I've never had to set aside my emotions to do what's right. I've survived worse things. And through it all, I've fought and clawed my way to where I am now without compromising my integrity.

I can do this. I can let go.

ELEVEN

Caitlin

Everyone but Jordan is in the living room when I come down the next morning, the presents all pulled from under the tree so Dad can start distributing them. Piper probably has over twenty presents alone and already she's gotten into the whole spirit, a polka dot pink and white bow on top of her head. Mrs. Rowe is wearing one, too, which makes it pretty easy to figure out who started it. Holiday music is playing from the speakers and I can smell the scent of chocolate chip cookies and hot chocolate wafting from the kitchen. Everyone is here but Campbell and Jordan.

I try my best to be casual about their absence, my heart beating a mile a minute as I join them in the living room in my pajamas. *Did Jordan kick him out?*

Do they know?

But no one says anything, not when everyone's busy

talking at the same time. Mr. Rowe is holding Piper on his lap while his wife makes funny faces to make her laugh, Addison is on the floor arranging the presents by recipient while Dad hands them to her one by one. Mom sits behind Dad taking pictures of the whole thing, still using an old camera Jordan and I gave her five years ago.

"Where's Campbell?" I finally ask and Dad looks up.

"He left last night. He told Jordan something came up. What it was is anyone's guess," he says.

"So you talked to him before he left?"

"Oh, no," Mom says. "We were asleep by then. He and Jordan were playing their video games in the bonus room. You know how they are."

"I just hope his boss doesn't have him working on Christmas day," Dad says as he hands the first present from beneath the tree to Piper who grasps it in her pudgy hands and shakes it around happily. Addison laughs, pulls out her phone and starts taking pictures.

"So he didn't even sleep over? And Jordan, where is he?" I sit on the floor across from Piper, hoping no one can see the guilt written all over my face or tell that my voice is shaking.

Mom shakes her head. "Jordan says Cam left at around one in the morning. He's in the kitchen getting the–"

"Oh, good, you're finally up." Jordan enters the living room carrying a tray filled with mugs of hot chocolate and a plate of chocolate chip cookies. He sets it on the coffee table before handing a mug to Mom and another to Dad. "Campbell had to leave last night. He said something had come up and he had to leave."

"Did he say what it was?" I ask, noting that there's one less mug on the tray and it's all my fault.

Jordan shrugs. "All I know is that he got a phone call and that was that. I asked him what it was about, if it was work but he said it wasn't. He said he'd tell me later but he had to leave."

"He didn't even get to take his presents with him," Mom says.

"I don't think he'd have been able to find it even if he tried," Mr. Rowe says, chuckling. "Everything else is buried under Piper's presents."

Mom passes a mug of hot chocolate to Addison. "I just hope the poor boy's not working on Christmas Day."

"Isn't he supposed to be on vacation?" Addison asks as Jordan joins them on the floor and she takes pictures of him, too.

"It's definitely weird not having him here," Dad says, "but Campbell's an adult. He can do whatever he wants to do."

"Do you think he's seeing someone?" Addison asks

Jordan and my heart skips a beat when Jordan looks straight at me.

"What?" My voice is barely a whisper. Crap, he knows.

"Could you hand me a cookie, Cait?" he asks as I hand him one, my hand shaking. Why am I acting so guilty?

Piper shrieks happily as she shakes another present wrapped in a pink paper and a sparkly white bow and I force myself to stop thinking of Campbell or how much I miss him. It feels so different not having him here. But then, maybe if I hadn't slept with him, maybe he'd wouldn't have left. Nothing would have changed.

"Guess Piper's eager to open her presents. Everyone ready?" Dad asks and everyone nods in agreement, the signal that the O'Halloran Christmas Day tradition of opening presents would keep going—with or without Campbell.

Two HOURS LATER, with all presents opened and Piper testing everything by bringing it to her mouth to chew while Addison rushes with a wet wipe to make sure it's clean, everyone gets ready to leave. Mr. and Mrs. Rowe are headed to church and Jordan and Addison are headed back to the city with Piper. There's another party they need to go to later that afternoon, this time with the Rowes.

Since they can't take all the presents Piper received, some will remain in the house for the weekends when Mom and Dad babysit. There's also a group of new toys for the Rowes when they have Piper over at their house on the weekends they alternate. But they are taking the crocheted dolls Campbell bought which he'd labeled from both of us with a note, *Caitlin picked the boy with the beanie*, on the label.

My heart had skipped a beat when Addison read his card and label out loud in front of everyone, only to have my momentary high crushed when Jordan looked at me, surprised.

"You shopped together for this? When?" he had asked as everyone's attention turned to me. It didn't even matter if his question was innocent or not but I could feel my face turn a bright shade of red. Why did I feel like I'd just gotten caught doing something I shouldn't have done?

"What does it matter, Jordan? Piper likes it," Addison said before I could answer. "Maybe that's because the doll's a redhead like her and her daddy." As she kissed Jordan on the lips, I could have sworn my brother blushed but what mattered more was that he got too distracted to pursue the question about Campbell and me shopping together.

After we opened the presents, I helped with the cleanup and quickly retired to my room, busying myself with phone calls to wish friends a Merry Christmas. It felt like any other Christmas morning but it wasn't. For one thing, Campbell was absent.

An hour later, I watch Jordan arrange the toys in the back of the cab as Addison snaps Piper in her baby seat. Snow blankets the yard and up until last year, Campbell and I always ended up in a snowball fight.

The knock on the door snaps me back to the present and I turn to see Mom standing outside. "Hey, Cait, mind if I come in?"

"Of course not." I grab the laptop from my bed and set it on the desk as she steps inside. As she sits on the edge of the bed, I pick up the clothes on the floor, the ones I tried to toss into the hamper last night and missed.

"You've been quiet for most of the morning. Is everything okay?"

"Yeah. Just tired, that's all."

"It was really nice of you and Campbell to buy matching dolls for Piper," she says. "Handmade is always my favorite."

"It was his idea."

"I loved the presents he gave you. What were they?"

"Oh, they were nothing. A *Coriolanus* hardcover book that he got the performers to sign and a DVD of the live play."

Mom smiles. "That was really nice of him. But didn't you see it with that other guy? Malcolm?"

I sigh. I've never really lied to them about who I've been seeing but I haven't exactly been telling them the truth either. I deleted the message I'd left on the answering machine about staying at Campbell's for the night and never once corrected them whenever Malcolm's name came up.

"Mom, I'm not dating Malcolm," I say slowly. "Our date was actually a disaster. He ended up with someone else that night at the party."

Mom's eyes widen. "Oh, dear. Did he at least take you home? How come you never said anything when we saw you the next day?"

"Because Campbell was at the party, too, and I spent the night at his place. He took the couch and I had the bed. It was also raining cats and dogs," I reply.

"I remember. Your Dad and I were stuck in New Jersey, too. He didn't want to drive so late at night, definitely not during the holidays."

"The next day, we went to the holiday market and that's where we found the dolls. After that, he dropped me off and invited me to see *Coriolanus* with him. His boss had given him tickets the night before."

"How come you didn't say anything about it? Your dad and I kept thinking you saw it with Malcolm."

"Because I didn't know how Jordan would take it,

me and Campbell hanging out together like that. I mean, we were just friends then."

Her eyebrow shoots up. "Then? What does that mean?"

"After *Coriolanus*, we kinda... hooked up."

Mom frowns, perplexed. "You... what?"

"We had sex... like, real sex." I bite my lip, feeling my cheeks turn warm. "And we were kinda together the other night, too, after having dinner with Jordan and Addy."

Mom looks at me with a stricken expression on her face. "Oh, dear."

"But I told him we were over," I add quickly, "that whatever we had wouldn't work out because I didn't want to risk his friendship with Jordan, or his relationship with our family. It was just a one-time thing and it's not going to happen again."

"What exactly is not going to happen again?"

I feel all color fade from my face. Jordan!

Getting up from the bed, I face an angry Jordan standing outside my door, a pair of felted owl slippers in his hands. From the look on his face, I don't need to answer his question. He heard everything.

Mom stands up to face him. "Jordan..."

"Addison packed these by mistake and I came up here to give these to Caitlin," he says angrily, tossing the slippers on the bed. "I can't believe you slept with him.

What the hell, Cait? What were you thinking? How could you jeopardize all the years–"

"And that's why we ended it," I counter. "We're over, Jory. We're over. It was just those two times."

"Those two times? It shouldn't have started in the first place, Cait!" Jordan pauses, muttering under his breath. "And Campbell should have known better."

"Jordan, we're both adults," I say. "We're not kids that you get to decide what we should do or don't do."

"How convenient. He's been my friend for years, Cait. He's been a part of our family for years. *Years.*" Jordan paces up and down the hallway. "No wonder he left the way he did, like a fucking thief in the night. He probably couldn't face me knowing what happened. He could barely look me in the eye last night."

Suddenly he stops his pacing and stares at Addison standing at the top of the stairs. Her expression soft, her energy calm. It's one of the things I like about her. She can calm him with just a look.

"Cait and Campbell slept together," he announces with a sigh. "I can't believe it."

Addison smiles faintly at me before turning her attention back to Jordan. "Piper's waiting in the truck with your dad. Why don't we talk about it on the way home?"

Jordan takes a deep breath, as if he's about to say something but he stops. His shoulders sag and he shakes his head. Without saying another word, he and Addison make their way down the stairs and I can hear her talking, her voice soft and soothing, as if she didn't just witness her fiancé losing it at the top of the stairs.

Mom and I don't talk as we watch them walk back to the car where Dad is sitting in the back seat with Piper. He gets out as they approach and they talk for a few moments before Addison gets into the passenger seat and Jordan gets behind the wheel. As they drive away, I look away, my vision clouded by my tears.

It hits me all of a sudden, the stupidity of it all, the hiding, the lying. And for what?

"I'm so sorry for messing up Christmas, Mom," I wail. "Jory's right. I should have known better."

Mom wipes the tears from my cheeks. "I don't know about Jordan being right about you and Campbell knowing better. Besides, you two have always gotten along great together. Ever since you were kids."

"You're not angry? Disappointed?"

"Why would I be? You and Campbell are adults. He's always been protective of you and I always thought it was cute," she says. "So things change. Do you like him, at least?"

"Mom, I slept with him, didn't I?"

She chuckles as she pulls away, wiping away my tears with her fingers. "That's not really an answer, Cait, but you don't have to answer right now."

I start crying in earnest again. "I just ruined a friendship, Mom. He's always been like a brother to Jory and look what just happened! Now he's upset."

"Jordan may be upset right now but I'm sure he'll also realize that you and Campbell are two consenting adults." She pushes a lock of hair behind my ear. "And that his baby sister is all grown up."

"Aren't you even upset?"

She smiles. "Oh, honey, you and Campbell are like two peas in a pod, and honestly, your dad and I have always wondered what was taking you two so long."

TWELVE

Campbell

THE MAN IN FRONT OF ME DRUMS HIS FINGERNAILS against the table between us. He's older now, graying at the temples, with wrinkles lining his forehead and the corners of his eyes. Funny how much I yearned for this moment ever since he abandoned us twelve years ago only to almost miss his call because I thought it was work, a local number I didn't recognize.

When I finally answered the call, I almost fell off my chair and had to make my way to the living room to take it. Jordan knew better than to eavesdrop. He simply continued playing the game although when I started to get dressed, he was right there, wanting to know if everything was alright. I wish I could have told him but I didn't know where to begin. I just wanted to know if it was real. It could have been the world's cruelest joke.

And so here we are at the Midtown hotel he's

staying at. The bar's closed and except for the two people behind the check-in desk, there's no one else in the lobby. We could go up to his hotel room and talk but I also want something neutral. I'm on guard in front of my own father.

After all, it's been twelve years since he left. Twelve years since he pretended he wasn't married or had a son who kept wondering what the fuck he did wrong that his own father would simply desert him without even a letter? Mom and I lost everything because of him, even the house that I loved so much.

I take a deep breath. So why am I here? Is it because I want bygones to be bygones? Is it because I realized when looking at the tree that's in my living room every night since Caitlin talked me into putting one up, that I've been holding on to my anger ever since he left us with nothing? Is it why I keep every woman at arms' length, never letting them close for fear that I'd turn out like him?

He'd fallen in love with someone else, a woman he said was smarter than Mom, a fellow ad rep for the company he worked for. They'd been sleeping together for a year, all his excuses about needing to work late at the office nothing but lies. When she told him she wanted to set up her own ad agency, he went all in. That's why he forged my mother's signature and took out that second mortgage, giving his mistress every dime.

The divorce papers he served my mother almost broke her, the woman who made sure I had everything I needed even when she didn't have enough for herself. After the O'Hallorans took me in, assuring me and my mother that no one was using the guest room anyway—and that Jordan and Caitlin had promised to behave for the rest of the year (Caitlin apparently promised to pick up after herself), it was a no-brainer. Jordan also needed someone to tutor him in Algebra so he'd graduate and that's where I came in.

"Why are you here?" I finally ask, tired of seeing the past played out in my head. "What do you want?"

"I saw your picture in the papers last month and I wanted to stop by and tell you how proud I am of you."

"Is that all you came into the city to tell me?" I don't even ask him where he's living now. I don't care.

"I also want to apologize for what I did to you and your mother," he continues. "I have no excuse."

"I just need one reason. Just one."

His gaze drifts around the empty lobby before settling on his hands. "I don't know what to tell you, Campbell. I thought I was in love."

"You had a family, Dad," I say through gritted teeth. "Weren't we enough for you?"

"I don't know what I was thinking then, Campbell. I wish I could do things over again but what's done is done, and while I don't expect you or your mother to forgive me. I... I just want you to know I'm very sorry."

"What do you want me to do, Dad? Forgive you just because it's Christmas?" I ask, hiding my irritation. "After twelve years of not even wishing me a happy birthday once—hell, not even a Christmas card—you show up like this. You don't even have the decency to let me know ahead of time that you'll be in town? Instead, you call me in the middle of the night asking to meet just so you can tell me something you could have easily said in a letter or a phone call so many years ago."

He sighs. "I'm so sorry, Campbell. I... I wasn't so sure if you'd even agree to this."

"So you figured a midnight text message would do it?"

"I just... I just wanted to see you, that's all," he says, looking smaller than I remember him as he sits across from me. Or is it just the way I'm seeing him as I do my best not to let my anger get the better of me. He's not worth it, not after all the years I spent pushing myself so hard just so I would never feel helpless again... or homeless for that matter.

I ask myself why I haven't gotten up from the chair and headed home. There's no point going back to the O'Halloran's anyway, not when I know I won't be good company for the next few days after this hell of a surprise. But I also can't stay. I've seen him now and he's fine and that's all I need to know.

"Campbell, I..." Dad begins, taking a deep intake of breath as he looks down at the table before his gaze returns to my face. "I was hoping I could make it up to you. I want to reconnect. You and me."

I don't know why I'm suddenly angry but I am. "When the holidays are over, will you be gone then? Are you talking about an annual thing?"

He shakes his head. "No. Nothing of the sort, son. I... I just want us to reconnect. That's all. This past year, I've realized what a terrible father I've been."

"Try husband first. Then you can work on the father part," I say through gritted teeth. "What you did to Mom was unfair. She lost the house, Dad. Our house. Our home," I say, fighting the urge to get up and walk away. "You just can't expect all that shit you pulled on Mom and me to magically disappear just because one day—twelve years after you walked out on us—you had an epiphany that you were a horrible husband and father."

Dad's eyes look at me imploringly. "Campbell..."

I get up, wanting to be anywhere else but here with him. "You know what? Why don't you call me in three months and ask me again, alright? That way, I'll know you really mean it when you say you want to reconnect with me not just for one night but from here on," I say.

"Hell, I'm still reeling from the fact that you're sitting right in front of me convincing yourself that your walking out on us wasn't as bad as it was because I turned out alright. Well, I did, alright? And no thanks to you. So give me some time to figure all this out, okay? And if you're serious—really serious—then maybe you'll call me again and actually give me some notice that you'll be in town. Make it look like you actually planned it instead of the way it looks now, that I'm just a last-minute appointment to you because that's the way it looks."

I don't wait for Dad to reply, not that he can. He stares at me, his expression hurt. But this isn't about him, the man who walked out on us twelve years ago. This is about me and how I've allowed my father's abandonment of me dictate my hopes and dreams.

This is also about me needing to wal away, at least, for now. Sometimes it's better not to draw things out... not when there's nothing left to say.

Jordan's text message comes as no surprise the next morning. I knew it was coming. I'd prepared for it. I just don't expect the sense of relief that hits me and it's like a load that's lifted off my shoulders. It doesn't even matter that I've just lost the best thing that ever happened to me—my friendship with the O'Halloran family. After meeting my father a few hours ago, I'm too numb to feel anything else.

Jordan: WTF??? Is it true???

Three letters. It wouldn't have taken a rocket scientist to know that he's heard about what happened between Caitlin and me. It wouldn't have taken much for Caitlin to tell her family the truth, not that I'd have wanted her to keep up the pretense this long.

For as long as I've known her, she's a terrible liar. Cute as a button but a terrible liar nonetheless.

I set my phone down on the bedside table and go back to sleep. After my meeting with Dad, I'd gone home and sat in front of the Christmas tree, a glass of scotch in my hand. It's one of the habits I've acquired hanging out with the higher-ups who invite me to their private clubs to discuss business. They taught me the ways of Manhattan's elite, introduced me to the models Marissa had seen me hanging out with on social media, and allowed me the opportunity to taste flavors of orange and cinnamon spice in a certain whiskey and how, with the addition of water (not ice), even a hint of chocolate. But I would have traded all that for waking up at the O'Halloran home with the family, handed out presents and opened them, laughing and joking like a real family. By the time I crawled into bed, the sun had begun to rise.

But now the doorbell is ringing and there's no way I can go back to sleep. I get out of bed and make my way to the front door. I don't need to look through the peephole to know who it is. Only one other person is on the list of people allowed to come up without needing to be buzzed in.

"What the hell, man? Is it true? You fucking slept with my sister?" Jordan exclaims the moment I open the door and he barges in. I know better than to stand in front of him, stepping aside as he storms inside carrying a paper shopping bag.

"If you're asking me that question, then you know I did," I reply, rubbing my eyes. "And no, I didn't force her to do anything she didn't want to do. It was consensual."

He curses under his breath, pushing me against the wall. I can see his jaw clench. "I hope to God she isn't just one of your side chicks because I'm going to kill you myself if that's the case."

I push Jordan away and he takes a step back. "I thought you know me better than that, man. I'd never do that to her and unless you've got something else to say, we've got nothing else to talk about."

"Who ended it? This... this fling or whatever it is. She's been beside herself since this morning."

"She did. It was her idea," I reply, exhaling. "Satisfied? Because I'm done talking about this."

"These are your presents, by the way. They were already in the truck when I heard about it." Scowling, Jordan sets down the paper shopping bags on the floor.

"You didn't have to do that."

He exhales. "Look, Campbell, you're like a brother to me... but my sister? Come on! Do you like her, at least?"

My anger flares. "What kind of question is that, Jordan? Of course, I like her. I like her more than you know."

Jordan glares at me for a few moments before he takes another step back, exhaling. "Alright. Just checking."

"Look, you can say whatever you want. Punch me if you want, hell, I don't care. But it was over even before it started and I'm not going to push it. Cait wants to focus on her studies and if that's what she wants, then I have to take a step back." I lean my shoulder against the corner that juts out from the hallway to the living room. "I would never do anything to hurt her or your family. I had no intentions of playing around with her."

Jordan's brow furrows. "You really serious about that?"

"I've always respected Cait. You know that." Who the hell am I kidding? I've always liked her.

Jordan's eyes narrow. "You do know she's stubborn as hell, right? And that sometimes, she can't make up her mind?"

I chuckle. "Of course, I knew that. I wouldn't have expected any less from her."

Jordan walks toward me, resting his hand on my shoulder. "Look, Cam, you're family. You've always been family and I just hope everything will work out for the best between the two of you. Man, if any man can handle her, it's you but I'm also not going to tell you what you should do. If you guys don't work out, you and I will just have to cross that bridge when we get there. Right now, I have to accept that she's all grown up and that you know what the hell you're doing." He takes a deep breath. "I also don't want to lose both of you."

As I look into Jordan's eyes, I realize it must have taken a lot to say what he just said to me. But I also get it. He's caught between a rock and a hard place, between protecting his sister from getting hurt from the man he's known to date casually only because I could never open myself up to woman for fear that I'd turn out like my father.

And while he could have chosen to beat the crap out of me, I'm grateful he doesn't do that. I'm too tired to fight back anyway, too emotionally spent after seeing my father again after so many years spent wishing he'd actually see me or, at least, call. Funny that when he finally did, all I wanted to do was leave. He'd become a stranger to me, a ghost from my past that I need to walk away from.

"Thanks, man."

"You look like shit," Jordan says as he pulls me in a brief hug, patting my shoulder when I pull away. "So, what happened last night? Who called? My folks called your mom and she's fine."

"You wouldn't believe me if I told you."

Jordan's eyes narrow for a few seconds before he gets it, his eyes widening in surprise. "Hell froze over?"

I nod. "Yeah, after twelve years. I guess something good actually came out of that article that had me listed as one of the top twenty analysts in the country last month. He thought he'd stop by to tell me how proud he was of me."

Jordan snickers. "How convenient of him. What took him so long?"

I shrug. "Who knows?"

"Where is he now?"

"I don't know and I don't want to know." I pause, frowning. "It's sad that everything I did to get to where I am today was driven by that need to be appreciated and to be acknowledged by him. I carried his rejection of me so much that sometimes I couldn't remember why I did things. Was it for me or him? And when that moment finally came, when he finally showed his face to tell me he was so proud of me, I didn't feel any different. I didn't feel satisfaction. I felt nothing. It's probably how he felt about Mom and me when he left us. Nothing. Unfortunately, that doesn't make me any different from him, does it? The apple doesn't fall far from the tree."

Jordan doesn't say anything for a few moments. He studies my face, his eyes searching. "Cam, listen to me. Everything you've achieved, you did it because you knew what you wanted and you went after it. Your degree, your career… everything." He pauses. "Still, just because you didn't feel anything when you saw him again doesn't make you just like him. You're different. And you wanna know just how different you are from him?"

"How?"

"Never once have you forgotten what matters," he says, tapping my chest with his knuckles. "Never once did you forget family."

THIRTEEN

Caitlin

"I can't believe you hid all this from me all this time." Roxy glares at me from the foot of my bed. She's stopped by the house to drop off her present only to get dragged up to my bedroom so I could pour my heart out to her. "I had a feeling you were hiding something from me but... but Campbell?"

"What's wrong with Campbell?"

"Nothing! You know why I never paired him with anyone?"

"Because he canceled both times?"

Roxy rolls her eyes. "Because I could tell no one was good enough for him. That man makes six figures a year and he's smart and gorgeous and kind. He also lives in Midtown which is a huge plus with all my nurse friends since the hospital is just Uptown." She holds up her forearm. "I had a list of friends this long who wanted to be paired with him. But do you know what his real problem was?"

I shake my head. "He's too busy?"

"He was never available for any one of my matches. Ever. I tried, Cait," she says. "But do you know who he always had time for when it came to hanging out?"

"Jory?"

"You!" She exclaims. "He always made time for you."

"He makes time for Jory more."

"Jordan's a guy so he doesn't count. They do guy things together. They play video games or shoot hoops or whatever. They don't go shopping at the holiday market all day or have drinks at some fancy schmancy place and then see a play." She peers at me suspiciously. "Are you sure there's nothing wrong with your guy-dar?"

"My what?"

"Your guy radar," she replies as she finally sits on the bed. "Come on, Cait. Campbell has liked you forever. And you know why I know? Because he never made time for my two matches for him even when he told me he wasn't seeing anyone at that time. He always had an excuse."

"I'm sorry for your two friends."

"That's okay. They were never his type," she says. "But you're his type. That's why he always makes time for you. Come on, Cait, he set up a Christmas tree in his apartment because you asked him to, for Pete's sake. Any man who does that for a woman does it because he likes her."

I blush, remembering the things we did in front of that tree. "I kinda figured that out after a while."

"Anyway, admit it, Cait. You messed up. Big time. But I only do the matchmaking. I don't do the stuff that comes after. Too complicated."

I roll my eyes. "Thanks."

"But you'll figure it out. You got yourself into this mess without my help. You can get yourself out of it." Roxy brings the rum-infused chocolate bar I'd given her for Christmas to her nose and inhales deeply. "Now that's my kind of chocolate!"

Fifteen minutes later, Roxy leaves so she can get ready for her shift. As crazy as she can be, she's right. I messed up—big time. And for what? Because I was afraid that if we did pursue the mutual attraction and it wouldn't work out, that it would ruin his friendship with Jordan and our family? Am I that scared of taking a chance on something that has never felt so right? And even I have to admit, whether he's Jordan's friend or not, Campbell has always been there for me for as long as I can remember, always supportive no matter what. And I trust him. There's no other man I've ever felt comfortable with, whom I can be my geeky and nerdy self with but Campbell Murphy. Just because I never allowed myself to appreciate the grown up parts of him before that morning after the holiday party doesn't mean I never did. I just never focused on it because he was my Jordan's best friend. I didn't want to mess anything up. I didn't want to hurt anyone.

By the time I make it to Campbell's apartment, it's mid-afternoon. The city is blanketed with snow and there's this happy feeling all over. But my happiness is clouded by doubt. *What if he's not home? What if he says no?*

But there's only one way to find out and that's what I'm doing. If anything, at least, he gets to hear my apology.

With the doorman announcing my arrival to him in a phone call, Campbell is waiting at the door the moment I step out of the elevator. My breath quickens and my heart rate speeds up. The sight of him makes my stomach clench and the butterflies residing inside flutter to life. What kind of sorcery is this? I've been with other guys before but none of them have made me feel this way—at least, not all sensations happening at the same time.

Giddy, that's the word.

"Come in," he says, stepping aside as I enter. He's

wearing a fitted black t-shirt and gray sweat pants. "Let me take your coat."

"I... I wasn't planning on staying long."

"Okay." He closes the door behind me and as I stand at the end of the hallway, careful not to track mud on his carpet, I see the tree all lit up. In front of it is a gift bag I last saw Jordan carry to his truck. Oh shit.

I check to make sure Campbell's not sporting any bruises as he stands in front of me. "Are you okay? Did Jory hurt you?"

Campbell smiles and shakes his head. "Nah, he's not that dramatic. He just dropped off the presents."

"And everything's fine? You're sure about that?" I ask, my panic growing. I want to inspect every inch of him to make sure my brother didn't touch a hair on his head or he'll never hear the end of it from me. "He said something about killing you when he found out."

"Guess he changed his mind."

"I didn't mean to tell him about us but he overheard me telling my mom," I stammer. "I didn't mean to tell her either but... but she thought I saw the play with Malcolm and I had to correct her and that's when Jory overheard us."

"And I'm glad he did, Cait, because I would have told him myself if you hadn't told him first. Besides, we didn't break any laws by being together," he says calmly.

"Addy must have talked to him."

Campbell shrugs. "Maybe. Or maybe he understands that we're both adults and whatever happens, he trusts us enough to work it out ourselves."

I can feel perspiration gathering along my brow. "I'm sorry for the things I said to you last night. I was just scared and I didn't want to hurt anyone. And the more I thought about it, it just kept building up in my head until I felt I had no choice but to end it."

Campbell smiles. "Would you like to remove your coat? You're starting to sweat."

"Oh. Sure," I shrug off my coat and hand it to him.

"Your boots? I don't want you tracking mud all over my carpet."

"Sorry." I follow him back toward the door to slip off my boots while he hangs my coat behind the door. "I'm not interrupting you or anything, am I?"

"I was just getting ready to open my presents." He smiles and gives me a playful wink. "Want to keep me company?"

I smile, relief washing over me. "I'd love to."

"But before we do that, I was just about to prepare myself some hot chocolate? Want some?"

My grin becomes wider. "Sure. Can I help?"

"Of course."

I follow Campbell into the kitchen. It feels like we're getting our bearings somehow, doing something we always did together only this time, it's on totally new territory. There's just us this time and maybe even a whole new ritual.

He already has the ingredients on the counter. Dutch-processed cocoa powder, almond milk, finely chopped semi-sweet chocolate and sugar. He even has chocolate chip cookies cooling on a wire rack on the counter.

"Guess you weren't kidding. You could set up the phone over there and film the whole thing for social media."

He laughs. "Let's not and say we did." Campbell turns on the stove to heat the water already in a saucepan. "The whipped cream is the refrigerator, in case you want it."

Ten minutes later, we settle on the faux lambs wool rug in front of the Christmas tree with our mugs of hot chocolate on a tray next to a saucer of cookies. I can't believe he hasn't opened his presents yet but I'm also glad he hadn't.

The first present he opens is from my parents and we don't even have to guess. A pair of pajamas, although this one doesn't have cute animals all over it. Instead, it's blue plaid. All grown up, it seems. Jordan and Addison gave him a bottle of Bunnahabhain 12 Year, a 12-year-old single malt whiskey from the most Northern distillery on Islay, and from Jordan personally, a pair of wool socks with llamas all over it. Must be an inside joke because Campbell laughs, shaking his head, the whole time he looks at them. The last present is from me and I find myself wishing I'd gotten him something more meaningful. But it was something I'd ordered before I flew home, delivered to the house before I ran into him at the party.

Campbell laughs when he pulls out a desktop golf game from the box, complete with putter that swung from a triangular base, a magnetic flagpole and a putting surface that he can adjust to change the pitch of the green and putt a different hole every time. The flagpole also serves as a way to retrieve the ball from the cup.

"This is genius," he says, unwrapping the parts and putting his first hole. "Thank you, Cait. This is exactly what I need when I need to decompress at work."

"You're welcome."

"I got you something, too." He reaches for a small bag from underneath the tree and hands it to me. It's small and light.

"But you got me the owl slippers and the signed *Coriolanus* stuff."

"So? Doesn't mean I can't get you anything else." When I don't answer, he continues. "Open it."

I tear the wrapper to see a silver box. I pause, eyeing him suspiciously but he only winks at me.

I lift the lid, grinning from ear to ear when I see what's resting inside, the molecular structure for dopamine cast in solid platinum with its chemical bonds represented in ruby, my birth stones.

"It's how you've always made me feel," Campbell says. "Good."

"Oh, Campbell," I say, picking up the necklace and holding it up. "You know me so well."

"I figured you'd get it. Would you like me to put it on you?"

"Yes, please." I hand him the necklace and he fastens the chain behind my neck before kissing the top of my shoulder gently, an almost effortless reaction that catches us by surprise.

"Turn around, Cait." I don't even think about it. I just do it, turning around to face him because he asked me to, our faces so close together, our lips so tantalizingly close. I suddenly feel dizzy. No, not dizzy. I'm giddy and I want us to keep going. No more second thoughts. No more doubts.

"Kiss me," I whisper and he does, a slow and lingering kiss that begins as a brush of our lips, tingles running up and down my spine as the pressure deepens. When he pulls back, I feel lost, wanting to feel his kiss again. "What's wrong?"

"Is this what you want, Cait?" His voice is a hoarse whisper. "Because I don't want to play any more games. I want the real thing."

"I don't want to play games either. I like you more

than you'll ever know, Campbell Murphy, and for much longer than you care to know. Heck, more than I was willing to admit to myself."

"And now?"

"I'm admitting it," I reply. "I like you and I'd like us to keep going."

He waits for a few moments, his eyes narrowing. "Why do I have a feeling that there's a 'but' waiting at the end of that sentence?"

"I've got one more semester."

He chuckles. "And? You don't think I can wait?"

"And then I have to find a job and take whatever comes along."

"I like you with or without a job, Miss O'Halloran. As long as you're happy doing whatever it is you want to do, I'll always be here for you. Not just as a friend, but as something more," he says. "But I can't do it alone. You have to trust me, too. You have to trust us."

"But what if we don't work out? Will you still be friends with Jordan? With the family?"

"But what if it does work out, Cait? What then?" he asks. "Will you let your fear take over and leave you wondering what if? Or will you take that chance with me and tell yourself, why not?"

"You're really good at this."

"I'm really better with numbers, but numbers don't kiss back. They don't taste as good as you."

I blush, his gaze reminding me of one of Roxy's words, *panty-melting*.

"So what will it be, Cait?"

"Yes. Yes to everything."

"Good." A smile brightens Campbell's features, his eyes crinkling at the corners. Outside, it has grown dark and the only light in the living room is from the tree, its string lights dancing gold and white.

"I hope you didn't have any plans to go home," he murmurs as he draws closer, "because I'd hate to take you home right now."

I feel his lips brush against mine, soft and warm, stubble grazing my chin. "I wasn't exactly planning on it."

"I was hoping you'd say that," Campbell murmurs. "The weather's not exactly a let's-hang-outdoors kind of weather."

"No, it's more why-don't-we-hang-out-by-the-fireplace kinda weather."

He grins. "Electric fireplace work for you?"

"Of course," I whisper as he continues to kiss me, his stubble against my neck making me giggle. "Anything with you in it will work for me, actually."

He pulls away, amused. "Really?"

"Yes, really."

"I like the sound of that, Cait. I'm glad the feeling is mutual."

FOURTEEN

Campbell

FIVE MONTHS LATER

Thanks to crazy LA traffic, I almost miss seeing Caitlin walk across the stage to accept her diploma. But of course, I don't, not if Jordan can help it. He's waiting for me outside the school campus gate and as soon as the Uber driver drops me off, we hurry to the building where the commencement ceremony is going on.

Luckily, as New Yorkers, we're both so used to walking that we make it inside the auditorium just as the Dean starts announcing names starting with M. The moment we hear her name from the loudspeakers, we applaud and cheer as loud as we can, Jordan and I whistling for good measure. We don't even care that people look at us funny. I know it's a formal affair but it's more than just years of hard work for Caitlin. It's years where the O'Halloran family sacrificed so much to get her the best education she deserved.

She's also officially my girl.

As Caitlin walks across the stage, I can't believe how proud I feel. She looks so radiant in her cap and gown and when she looks up at us causing a ruckus in the audience, her beautiful face cracks into a wide smile before she turns her attention back to the Dean, her expression all serious now as she accepts her diploma.

And just like that, she's officially got her Masters in Molecular Biology.

"That's my girl," I say, whistling.

"No, that's my sister, man," Jordan says as Addison just rolls her eyes, as if saying nope, they haven't changed one bit.

Hard to believe there'd been times when I found myself seriously doubting if Caitlin and I would ever work out in the long term. Maybe she was right at the dinner table that Christmas Eve, when she talked about holiday romances being so fleeting, lovers' emotions too caught up in the season.

But then, Caitlin and I didn't just meet during the holidays. We've known each other since we were kids which means our foundation is strong. And we weren't exactly just sitting around doing nothing either. We were both busy—sometimes too busy. She had that dissertation and other graduation requirements to complete and I had work and the crazy hours that come with it. There's also a job offer from a hedge fund that I seriously need to make a decision on, but not until I talk to Caitlin first.

And then there was the issue of my father who meant it when he said he wanted to reconnect with me. Realizing I needed to recover from the initial shock of seeing him again, he asked to meet me in February and then in March. A talk over coffee one day and lunch the next, we're starting to get to know each other again. It'll be a slow road between us but it's a start.

Half an hour later, after Caitlin introduces me to her friends and professors and smiling for all the pictures, we make our way toward the house the O'Hallorans are renting a few blocks away from the university. We could have gone to some posh restaurant to celebrate but this is what Caitlin wants, to be able to kick off her high heels and be around family.

The weather is perfect for a leisurely stroll and on the way, Jordan orders Thai food to be delivered complete with Thai iced teas, coffee, and fried bananas with coconut ice cream for dessert. He's still pulling my carry-on luggage, insisting I need to keep my hands free for his sister anyway.

And I'm glad for that because I can't get enough of Caitlin although I keep it at handholding for now. The rest can come later.

With her graduation gown and cap now folded and tucked away, she looks stunning in her sleeveless V-neck fitted dress. I don't even know what color it is. Taupe? It reminds me of sand but more importantly, it makes Caitlin's red hair and her freckles stand out.

"For a minute there, I thought you wouldn't make it," she says as I loosen my tie, my jacket draped over my other arm. I didn't want to appear too casual for her graduation but I clearly underestimated the casual culture of Los Angeles. Even Jordan and his dad are wearing button down shirts and chinos.

"I wouldn't have missed it for the world, Cait. Too bad I had one more deal to close at the office before I could fly out."

"I'm glad you're here. I could hear you and Jory all the way from the stage," she says, giggling. "You guys were loud."

"New Yorkers are loud. Or have you forgotten?" I tug at her hand playfully, wrapping my arm around her as she turns toward me. "I've missed you, Cait."

"I've missed you, too, Campbell." We stop walking and kiss, the scent of her making my nostrils flare. A car honks its horn at us.

"Get a room!" Someone yells, laughing as Caitlin pulls away and we continue to walk.

"Do you really have to leave in two days?"

"I have to finish up some work before..." My voice

fades. Any more talking and I'll ruin the surprise. "Well, before we close another deal."

"All work and no play makes Campbell a dull boy, you know."

I chuckle. "Let's hope not. Anyway, I met someone while playing golf last week. He owns an investment firm just a few blocks from my office and he offered me a position. It's similar to what I'm doing right now, only I'll be working for a hedge fund."

Caitlin frowns. "Were you even looking?"

"I'm not, but ever since that feature last year where I was named among the top analysts in the country, I get a call now and then," I reply. "It doesn't hurt to check out what they've got to offer."

Caitlin looks at me expectantly. "And?"

"It turns out he knows Addison and Jordan."

"How?"

"He's Addison's friend's father-in-law. Daniel Drexel and he owns an investment firm. Hedge funds."

"Really? Does she know?"

I nod. "He and his son are among the investors in the expansion of her medical practice."

Caitlin laughs. "What a small world!"

"I received his formal offer on my way here."

She turns serious. "Wow, that's serious, Cam. Does it pay more? Is that why you're considering it? Although if it means you're going to end up working longer hours than you already do—"

"That's the thing, Cait. I won't," I reply. "The hours are more consistent. Market hours."

Caitlin's eyes narrow. "What does that mean? You already work almost a hundred hours sometimes when there are deals closing."

"I'll probably spend about sixty to seventy hours a week. It beats the usual seventy I spend now that usually turns into a hundred hours when it's time to close the deals."

"A hundred hours a week is a lot, Cam. I always knew you worked long hours. I just had no idea how long," she says.

"I get holidays."

"I didn't mind it as much when we were living apart but now that I'm moving back to New York, what then? Will I even see you? Or do I have to wait until a holiday break?"

I squeeze her hand. I'd told Mr. Drexel that the only reason I'd consider his offer was if I got to keep market hours and he agreed. He said he commuted to see his family in New Mexico for years while running his business. Sure, he had a partner but he believed in family coming first. It's rare to hear such words coming from a co-executive managing member of a global investment management firm but everything I've read about him and his company seem to measure up. He's a widower now, his wife having died from cancer years ago.

"I've spent the last 48 hours studying everything about his company. He's been in investing for about twenty years and his record is solid. His connections are..." I pause, exhaling as I remember the details about Mr. Drexel. The man was a lifetime member of one of the most exclusive men's clubs in New York. "Let's just say he knows the right people."

"So you have a good feeling about him?"

I nod. "But I want your input as well. He wants me to fly to London to check out their international offices in a week but it's only a formality. If I take the position, I'll be in New York."

We've arrived at the house and the rest have gone inside but we remain standing outside the door. Caitlin bites her lower lip. "You sound like you're thinking about accepting the offer."

"Not without asking what you think about it first."

She thinks for a few moments. "What do you like about it the most?"

I pull her to me and kiss her softly on the lips. "I get to spend more time with you."

"It would be nice not to see you on my phone screen for a change. Besides, I like the original version better," she says, smiling. I love how her eyes sparkle when she's happy, and right now, those green eyes sure are sparkling.

"I wish I could help you move out of your apartment," I murmur.

"Jordan is going to help me," she says. "And I also don't have much. The apartment came fully furnished and a student is moving into my room as soon as I leave."

"If you need me to help you before I leave, I can do that."

"I'm taking you all around LA the next two days, Cam, remember? The Hollywood sign, Grumman Chinese Theater, the Getty Center, so no moving stuff until after we do the Hollywood tourist thing. Oh, and I'll be sneaking out of the house to be with you at your hotel."

"That's more like it," I say, chuckling. "I aim to do bad things with you, young lady."

Caitlin looks around to see if anyone from her family is around but they're all inside already. She takes a step closer, our noses touching playfully. "And I aim to please, Mr. Murphy."

I wrap my arms around her waist, one hand dropping down the curve of her ass. "That'll be Sir to you later."

She giggles as I kiss her, pulling away only when a car stops in front of the house and the driver and his passenger emerge with plastic bags filled with what looks like our food order. "Goodness, just how much food did Jordan order?" Caitlin asks as she takes a step toward the front door.

"Looks like the whole menu," I say, laughing as I allow her to pull me inside the house, the sounds of her family moving about and getting the table ready reminding me that unofficially—for now—they're my family, too.

FIFTEEN

Caitlin

Two weeks later, I see Campbell in the crowd, a gorgeous dark-haired man standing a head taller than most of the people around him. My heart feels like it's about to burst out of my chest and the butterflies in my belly are fluttering like crazy. If this is what it's like to be in love, then I'm all for it. I just don't know why I waited so long.

"Campbell!" I rush into his arms, feeling him bury his face in my neck and hair.

"Hey there, beautiful," he murmurs. "How was your flight?"

"Long. But I'm not complaining," I reply. "Thanks for upgrading my ticket. First class is amazing."

"You're welcome."

I feel his lips against mine, warm and soft, the airport around us fading into the background. It's only been two weeks since I last hung out with him in LA when he joined my family to watch me walk across the stage and accept my diploma. Two weeks since we had so much fun playing tourist around LA and we have tons of pictures to prove it, many of them printed on photographic paper so we can frame them one day. He stayed with us for two days before he had to travel back to New York for work and from there, it took a week for me to pack up all my stuff at the apartment I shared with another grad student in Westwood. At least, Jordan got to stay behind and help me pack everything up and then accompany me on the flight back home.

How things have changed since my declaration about wanting to go straight to work as soon as I graduated. Ever since Campbell and I officially announced we were dating, it's as if real life finally hit me in the face (and my heart) and I realized life isn't all work and no play. Sometimes, it's okay to play. It's okay to set the job in the back burner and enjoy life for a while.

Heck, I don't even remember what my dissertation was about now, not right this minute, not when my world right now is right here with this man whom I've known since I was a child, the same man who's taking me on my first ever real vacation as his graduation present—to Italy, no less—even if I had to make the first part of my trip alone since he had to be in London a week earlier for work. But starting right now, this moment, it's just him and me in Venice, no less, the first leg of our trip.

While Jordan and my parents pooled their funds together for my graduation present, an all-expenses paid trip to Italy for two, it's Campbell who puts in the finishing touch. He upgraded everything from my flight to the accommodations. He's got everything planned and I can't wait.

The itinerary he's scheduled is amazing with enough time to rest and have fun in between. Definitely a lot of fun. Four weeks of exploring Venice, Florence, and Rome. There's even a lot of boating and sunbathing time in Positano, Capri, and the Amalfi Coast. Somewhere on that list is a four-day stay in Tuscany and I trust Campbell with the details. It's not his first time and so he knows exactly where to go, pulling favors from clients at work who got us the best hotel rooms and some of them even opened their private homes for us to use, villas and all. I don't even know where everything is exactly on the map he sent me after our last video call but I don't care. How could I think of going straight to work right after graduation and miss all this?

As Campbell pulls me closer, I can smell the scent of his cologne mingled with that man-smell of his that drives me crazy, with its hint of cinnamon and leather... even tobacco for someone who doesn't smoke. I also taste coffee on his tongue and the whole combination has my body vibrating. I pull away, suddenly embarrassed. We really need to get to a room, but not yet.

"We need to get my luggage."

Half an hour later, we're at the hotel which is in the Zattere area of Venice's Dorsoduro district overlooking the Lagoon. It's beautiful and I can't help but feel like I'm in a fairy tale, one that has my name on it.

"St. Mark's Square is just one water bus stop from here, pumpkin," he murmurs as he snaps a selfie of both of us with the Lagoon behind us. "I hope you packed your walking shoes."

"I brought two pairs, just in case," I reply, turning my head and kissing him on his bearded cheek. "I even brought a few stilettos for those fancy dinners you never fail to take me to."

He's already done his fair share of that and not once do I have to worry about towering over him. He's tall enough, confident enough and more than sexy enough to handle me.

Campbell looks at me knowingly, his eyes narrowing. "Really?"

"Yes, really," I whisper, biting my lip. "I know how you like to look at my legs."

"Oh, but it's not just your legs I like, Cait. I like all of you."

I turn around to face him, forgetting the phone that's probably still filming us as I wrap my arms around his waist and nuzzle his neck. "Thank goodness for that, because I'm the whole package, baby."

"Now we really need to get inside before we cause a commotion," he says, laughing as he tucks his phone back in his jacket and taking my hand, leads me inside the hotel.

We begin our official stay in the suite with a shower to wash off all the travel hours I've just logged. Too bad Campbell is more disciplined than I am for other than a long passionate kiss under the water spray, that's about it for any action in the shower. He orders me to wait and that's what I do. It's a side of him that he shows only to me and I love it. Commanding, domineering, and controlled.

"Get on the bed," he whispers in my ear as we leave the steaming bathroom, towels discarded on the floor along the way. "On your back, arms above your head."

I bite my lower lip, my heart racing as I do as I'm told. My hair is still damp from the shower but he lays a fresh towel underneath my head before proceeding to bury his face in my hair, his hands already exploring. Outside, it's getting dark, but there's really no rush for us to be anywhere else but right here.

"I missed you, Cait. You have no idea."

"Show me," I gasp as his kisses along my neck and shoulder make me shiver with excitement and need, his hands finding my breast and palming it, his thumb and index finger pinching and pulling my nipple. I want to hold him but I also know I can't. I never realized how obeying an order as simple as keeping my hands over my head could be so thrilling but with Campbell it is. I've always done what I wanted, but with him, all I want is to do what he wants me to do. He does it with a look, a touch, a whispered command.

Campbell's kisses continue down my breast and I moan as he takes a nipple in his mouth, licking it and sucking it as I squirm beneath him. He moves to the other nipple, squeezing my breast as his other hand trails along my side. His beard tickles my skin and his mouth and tongue, soft and warm, has me begging for more.

"So eager," he growls, his fingers finding me already wet for him.

"It's been two weeks, Cam." I grip the pillows above my head, turning my head to the side as I feel his other hand leave my breast to trail down my thighs, pushing them apart. I feel him breathe across my delicate skin and I moan. "It's been too long."

When his tongue slides across my sensitive lips, I'm lost. And this is just the beginning. This is just Campbell getting started. Like everything he does, he does it well and making love to me, making me feel like I'm the only woman in the world for him, is one of the things he does so well. It's a package deal and I feel like I've won the lottery of life with this man. But even as my mind says it's too soon for me to think such things, I don't care.

"You taste like heaven, Cait," he murmurs, his tongue stroking between my folds, curling and flitting across my slit. I grip the sheets, my gasps and moans filling the room. I don't want to be too loud that I'd wake up the neighbors. It happened once when he flew to LA to visit me and we took a weekend trip to Santa Barbara and we stayed at a resort known for its hiking trails. I was so noisy that the guest banged on the walls, but as embarrassed as I felt at that moment, Campbell and I laughed it off, giggling all throughout dinner afterward. He upgraded our accommodations then and got us our own little casita on the property where I could make as much noise as I wanted. Of course, I didn't but I was still loud enough. And the little house was all ours that weekend.

"Play with yourself, Cait," he murmurs as he drags his tongue up and down my slit, his fingers sliding in and hitting that sensitive spot. "Let me see you."

I cry out as the rush of sensations hits me, my hands finding my breasts, my fingers pinching and pulling my nipples. Campbell buries his face between my legs, his beard scratching the insides of my thighs as I come, my cries filling the room. He moves up across my body, his mouth meeting mine hungrily and I can taste myself on his lips, his tongue, feel the head of his cock rest between my folds, coating himself with my wetness. I reach for him, one hand on the back of his shoulder and the other, along his lower back, pulling him to me.

"Cait..."

Campbell groans, his thick cock pushing between my slippery folds, claiming me inch by inch as he watches my face with heavy lidded eyes. He pulls back, leaving only the head inside and I dig my nails along his back, gritting my teeth.

"Fuck me, Cam," I breathe as he drives his cock inside me and I cry out, loving the feel of him filling every inch of me. He buries his head against my neck as he begins to move, deep, hard strokes of his body that leaves me quivering, shaking beneath him. I can feel myself clenching around his cock, his mouth finding the perfect spot just behind my ear and slowly, ever so slowly, sucking the skin there until I feel myself shatter, all the sensations coming together in one thunderous spark.

"Come for me, Cait," he whispers. "Come."

And I do, my body shuddering as I feel myself shatter before him. I feel his fingers dig into the skin of my hips, holding me there as he drives his cock deep inside me, pumping me hard until his own release comes and he groans, his mouth against mine as he breathes my name.

"Cait..."

Moments later, I feel him shift on the bed, his arms circling my waist as he pulls me closer to him, my back molding perfectly along his torso. I feel his breath warm over my shoulder.

"I love you, Caitlin O'Halloran," he whispers, planting a kiss on my shoulder. "You have no idea how much I love you, and just how much I've missed you these past two weeks."

"I love you like crazy, too, Campbell Murphy," I whisper, turning to look at him. "I don't know why I waited so long to find out that you're a wild man in the sheets."

"That's because you bring out the animal in me."

I giggle. "I like that."

"Me, too."

"Do you think we were loud?"

He thinks for a moment. "The walls here are a lot thicker than back home. So, no, I don't think so." He pauses. "At least, I hope so."

"Campbell!"

He chuckles, nuzzling my neck again. "It's thick enough, Cait. Don't worry. This is the first of many accommodations on this trip. We'll find out soon enough if they're all thick enough. After all, my goal is to hear you scream my name every time I make love to you."

"Campbell Murphy, you're making me blush."

"Ah yes, and don't I love it when you do," he says,

his tone turning serious. "I love you, Caitlin O'Halloran."

"And I love you, Campbell Murphy." I roll onto my back and face him, loving the way he makes me feel so safe and so loved. As he pulls me closer, his mouth meeting mine, there's also no denying that I've loved Campbell for as long as I can remember. I just didn't know it then, all because he was my brother's best friend.

Only this time, he's mine. All mine.

Just as I've always been his.

All his.

Two and a half weeks later, standing on our hotel balcony overlooking the town of Positano at dusk and feeling a bit sunburned and tipsy, I find myself hating that it's almost over. In four days we head back home and Campbell goes back to work and I start my job hunt. At this rate, I'm going to need a serious vacation from this vacation.

I haven't even thought about work at all throughout the whole trip. I don't remember that self-righteous talk about getting a job as soon as I graduate because I want to start earning my way blah blah blah. All I know is that I want to spend the rest of my life with the only man I've ever loved since I was a little girl.

Even though we're supposed to be on vacation, we find ourselves talking about our future. We've talked about my plans to find work as soon as possible, even my original plan to move wherever the job is. So far, I have two job offers. Both of them are on the West Coast but right now, it's the last place I want to be, not when I want Campbell in my future and there's no way our relationship can survive long distance.

"What are you thinking, love?" Campbell asks as he stands behind me, wrapping his arms around my waist. Below us, the sound of the surf is intoxicating, the sight of the lights dotting the darkening hillside reminding me just how lucky I am to have found the love of my life.

"I'm thinking about how this moment is so perfect I wish I could bottle it and take it home with me," I whisper. "You, me, the town and all the steps we had to climb to get from here to there that one night."

"Ah, yes. But it was just that one night." As Campbell nuzzles my neck, I can feel his beard scratching my skin. He's forgone shaving for the last two and a half weeks and I have to admit, he looks so damn sexy that if I wasn't so tired from being on a boat most of the day swimming and snorkeling at the Blue Grotto and other places whose names I don't remember now, I'd ravish him right here.

"One night? Try wearing heels, dude," I say, remembering how we'd gotten lost two nights earlier trying to get to some restaurant on the other side of the town which would have given us an opposite view of the hillside. Only we'd made the wrong turn and had to walk two more blocks uphill and then downhill. But we found the restaurant and the view was just as beautiful as it was from our hotel balcony. The only difference was that from the restaurant, we could see *our* balcony.

"Are you complaining?"

"Hell, no. I wouldn't trade this whole trip for anything, Cam. I just wish I could bottle this perfect moment right now and keep it with me forever. You included," I whisper as a cool breeze kisses my skin and I close my eyes, feeling Campbell unwrap his arms from my waist and take a step away from me.

"Turn around, Cait."

I open my eyes and turn to face him, only he's not there, not standing in front of me, at least. No, he's down on one knee, a black box in the palm of his hand.

"Will you me marry me, Caitlin O'Halloran?" he asks. "Will you make me the happiest man in the world by being my wife?"

For a moment, my world seems to stop before my eyes. There's a deafening roar in my ears as my cheeks grow warm. In Campbell's eyes, I can see my life flash before me, from the moment I first became aware of the boy next door when I was a little girl up until I was in high school when I knew he was hurting after his father left but he kept it all inside. And then this, seeing him all grown up to the amazing man he's become, just as sunburned as I am but as handsome as ever with that ever-mischievous glint in his eyes.

Only this time, there's no mischief at all as he looks up at me. There's only love and the promise of a future together.

"Yes," I whisper as he takes my hand and slips the ring around my finger. "Yes, Campbell Murphy, I will marry you."

And as Campbell stands up and gathers me in his arms, his mouth covering mine in a deep kiss, I realize I don't just get to keep this perfect moment like I'd wished minutes earlier. I get to live it, too, with Campbell by my side.

Campbell

EPILOGUE

It's been two months since Caitlin moved in with me and I couldn't be happier. Sure, my life is still busy especially after I accepted Daniel Drexel's offer to join Drexel Marshall Capital Management LP as a senior analyst. He even had me fly to London to check things out just before I joined Caitlin in Venice. He needed someone to help run the London office and if I'd been single, I'm sure I'd have taken him up on it.

But the moment Caitlin became more than just Jordan's sister, things changed. My dreams certainly shifted, as well as the reasons why I used to pursue everything. Before Caitlin, life was about tackling the next big thing more to prove to my father that I was a better man than he could ever be than for myself. I didn't realize it until the moment I met him that night.

The pursuit of everything flashy had been for him more than anything. Finally meeting him again after all those years was like seeing an alternate version of myself if I'd kept going, the one that would never be happy with what he had... like family.

With Caitlin, I suddenly have a clearer picture of what I want and it's not a bigger high-rise apartment or a house in the Hamptons that'll be featured on some architectural magazine one day. It's not the fancy car or the memberships to the most exclusive clubs although I have to admit, they're nice. Instead, it's the simple things like dinners at home with friends and playing miniature golf with my best buddy (I figured I'd start small with Jordan before taking him to the golf course). It's the traditions I've learned to appreciate growing up next to the O'Halloran family from Christmas to birthdays to our upcoming wedding.

It's making sure I get home from work three times a week in time to enjoy Caitlin's dinners as she tries to perfect her skills in the kitchen while she continues sending her resumes out. It's waking up to the feel of her body nestled in my arms, the scent of her hair and the sleepy sound of her voice as she asks me to stay in bed five more minutes before I have to get ready for work. It's making love to her with everything I've got and feeling her surrender herself to me every time. It's knowing she trusts me completely just as much as I trust her.

I unlock the door to the apartment, catching the aroma of rosemary and balsamic vinegar in the air as I step inside and close the door behind me. Music plays from the speakers, jazzy vocals accompanying the view of the Empire State Building outside the window.

"Cam!" Caitlin rounds the corner from the kitchen and lands in my arms, her lips tasting of wine when she kisses me. "Welcome home."

As I pull her into my arms, I see that she's already set the table for two. That's what makes our intimate dinners even better than going to a restaurant. Where else can one have dinner in their PJ's with a view of the city before them? "I don't know what to devour first. You or whatever it is you're making. It smells amazing."

"It's Mom's recipe. Steak and potatoes with rosemary and balsamic vinegar," she says as I set the mail on the foyer console and my briefcase next to the couch. "It was the easiest one I could find. Not too many ingredients."

"I'm sure it'll be delicious." I've made it before and it's one of her mother's simplest recipes, flank steak with potatoes and rosemary, so I know she can't go wrong unless she burns it. "So how was your day, love?"

The smile fades from her face. "Still waiting to hear

from that company Addison recommended. I haven't heard from them yet and it's been a week."

"They could be contacting your references."

She pouts. "True, but I can't stand the waiting."

"All good things come to those who wait, grasshopper. Just look what I got when I waited for the right woman." I kiss the tip of her nose. "And she's damn fine if you ask me. Even better than I deserve."

A blush creeps on her cheeks, her pout replaced with a smile. "Oh, Cam. You really know how to make a woman feel better. Why don't you go get ready for dinner? I still have to make the salad."

"That's a good idea. Any more of this," I let my hand drift lower along her ass, "and I'll be having you for dinner."

She pushes me away playfully. "Go get ready, you. I won't have anything ruin this dinner."

"Not even sex?" I ask, loosening my tie. "We haven't tried it on the dining table yet."

"Oh, yes, we have. I've lost count," she says, her hands on her hips as she glares at me with one arched eyebrow.

"Drat! Foiled again," I say, chuckling as I make my way to the bedroom, everything about my workday fading away with each item of clothing I slip off... tie, shirt, belt. It's also a Friday which means we have the next two mornings to sleep in and burrow under the covers.

Twenty minutes later, I step into the living room and find her standing in front of the kitchen counter. As I approach, I see that she's got a piece of mail in one hand, the envelope torn open. In her other hand, she's holding a letter.

I stand behind her and wrap my arms around her waist, resting my chin on her shoulder. "Everything okay?"

"Cam, look." Her voice is shaking. Hell, she's trembling as she shows me the letter. "No, even better. Can you read it and make sure it says what I think it says?"

"What do you think it says?"

She turns to look at me. "Just read it. I don't want it all to be a dream."

"Is this from the company you want to work with?" I ask and she nods. I kiss the skin between her neck and shoulder, hoping she calms down soon but I also get why she's feeling this way. Caitlin is going stir crazy spending her days at the apartment or with her family. She wants to be busy, to work and contribute her skills toward something useful, especially one she spent the last four years studying. To top it all off, she'd prefer it to be in the East Coast which none of the job offers she's received are based out of.

Except one.

"Dear Ms. O'Halloran," I begin. "Following our recent discussions, we are delighted to offer you the position of Research Associate with–"

"It's an offer, right?" Caitlin asks excitedly as she turns around to face me. "It's an actual offer?"

"Yes, Cait, it's an offer which means my congratulations are in order," I say as she remains speechless, as if allowing the news to slowly finally sink in. "Now you'll need to write them a letter to let them know if you accept their offer or not."

"I'd be crazy not to accept it. It's in the city... well, New Jersey, but who cares? It means I don't have to move," she says. "Will you help me draft it? All I can think of saying is a long string of happy emojis."

I laugh. "No, that won't work, love. But I will help you draft a serious one."

"Thank you, Campbell." She wraps her arms around my neck. "I love you so much."

"And I love you more than you can ever imagine, Cait." I kiss her hair as I hold her, letting her process this next steps for as long as she needs.

A few seconds later, she pulls away, setting the letter on the counter. "We better start dinner before the food gets cold."

"You sure?"

"Yup," Caitlin replies as I follow her to the dining table and pull out a chair for her.

"Will you tell me about this position?" I ask as she's about to sit down. She stops and turns to face me, her eyes narrowing playfully.

"How much time do you have?"

I kiss her on the lips. "With you, Cait? Forever."

Curious about Caitlin's friend, Roxy?
*You can read her story in **Every Good Thing**!*

MEET ROXY AND KODI IN EVERY GOOD THING

What happens when you end up with your own trending hashtag?

For Roxy Porter, you try to salvage what's left of your nursing career by agreeing to billionaire Kodi Donovan's suggestion that they pretend to be engaged... just until the trend dies down.

But pretending to be something you're not, it turns out, isn't as easy as it looks... especially when feelings between them become real.

EVERY GOOD THING
PROLOGUE

I didn't mean to catch the bouquet. I'm single—have been since Jax and I broke up three months ago just as my best friend Caitlin O'Halloran and her brother's best friend Campbell Murphy started getting serious. If anyone deserves to catch the bouquet, it's Caitlin who was standing right in front of me, right in the path of that flying bouquet.

But, no. Caitlin stepped aside and before I could run as far away as I could, the bouquet landed in my arms and I almost got tackled by three very determined women.

And now here I am sitting on a chair in the middle of the dance floor while the man who caught the garter sheepishly gets down on one knee in front of me.

Poor guy. To have to rush to the church because he was one of the groomsmen right as soon as his plane landed at LaGuardia and then this, having to put the garter on my leg in front of all the guests.

Not that the guests at Addison Rowe and Jordan O'Halloran's St. Patrick's Day wedding are complaining... or at least, half of them aren't. The guests from the groom's side hoot and holler, cheering their buddy on while the bride's family and friends, especially her conservative and old-fashioned aunts, are too busy covering their eyes with their hands although they still manage to peek between their fingers.

It's going to be a train wreck. I just know it.

Or maybe not, considering Kodiak "Kodi" Donovan, the guy who caught the garter, is my best friend's brother's best friend. Tall with reddish hair and trimmed beard, some posh magazine called *Hamptons Live* voted him as one of New York's most eligible bachelors, and his nonprofit organization ReBuild to Heal was listed as one of the most successful organization in the country as of last year.

He's also way out of my league.

I lift my foot a few inches from the ground and as if on cue, he slips the garter up my ankle. His friends yell for him to slide it higher and as our eyes meet, I nod.

Knock yourself out, Kodi.

As the garter slowly makes it up my leg, the slit in my dress opens to reveal part of my thigh. Just a peek. Our friends cheer as the music stops and is replaced by something else. Kodi and I look at the each other, surprised at the song choice.

Whoever picked *The Stripper* by the David Rose Orchestra needs to burn in hell.

Higher! everyone yells.

Ay! Susmaryosep! the bride's aunts mutter under their collective breath, some of them still covering their eyes yet most of them still peeking. The uncles mostly stand and watch, amused.

Kodi turns his attention to me and with a wink, he slides the garter just above my knee. An inch, then another inch. He's taking his sweet time and the crowd is lapping it all up.

"You better push that thing above the knee or it'll be five years of bad luck for me," I say, feeling the slit of my dress slide open even more, my entire thigh now revealed before him. "Unless you're chicken."

It's a challenge and he knows it. Kodi grins as we lock eyes. We hold each other's gaze a beat longer than usual and my stomach clenches. I never realized how beautiful his eyes are.

Kodi's fingers feel warm against my skin as the garter slides higher, stopping along the middle of my thigh. He bites his lower lip, and it almost seems like he's about to push it even higher up my thigh but then he stops and that's as high as he goes. The crowd groans in disappointment. But then, who can blame him. There are children around, after all.

Everyone cheers as Kodi gets up and holds his hand out to me. The striptease music ends abruptly, replaced by something slow.

"I heard somewhere that the man who snags the garter is supposed to dance with the woman who catches the bouquet," Kodi says as I take his hand and he pulls me to my feet.

"Lucky you," I mutter, rolling my eyes.

He grins, guiding me across the floor effortlessly, his mouth in line with my ear. "Just how lucky will depend on you."

ACKNOWLEDGMENTS

Thank you so much to the following people for helping me get Campbell and Caitlin's story come to life.

Michelle Jo Quinn, for always being there for me, helping me see the forest for the trees when I get too lost inside my head with all the muses running around.

Charity Chimni, for cracking that virtual whip so I finish all the stories that I start and for all your valuable input and feedback.

To my awesome Reader Team: Suzanna Lusk Chriscoe, Belinda Bauknecht, Louise Hallett, Evelyn Martha, Jessica Cooper, Ellen Hawrylciw, and Lee Rey. Thank you for helping me bring Campbell and Caitlin's story to life!

ABOUT LIZ DURANO

Liz grew up devouring fairy tales and her mother's book collection (don't tell her!) that included Harold Robbins, James Clavell, and Colleen McCullough. Although she studied Journalism in college, she discovered that she preferred writing fiction and so these days, that's what she does. She writes women's fiction and romance and lives in Southern California with her family and a Chihuahua mix who keeps guard of her writing space.

You can follow Liz's book adventures by visiting lizdurano.com or follow her on Facebook at @lizduranobooks.

Let's Connect!
https://lizdurano.com
lizduranobooks@gmail.com

facebook.com/lizduranobooks

twitter.com/lizdurano

instagram.com/lizdurano

Printed in Great Britain
by Amazon